THE DUKE OF ACES

Ladies of Risk, Book 2

Rachel Ann Smith

ARE YOU SIGNED UP FOR DRAGONBLADE'S BLOG?

You'll get the latest news and information on exclusive giveaways, exclusive excerpts, coming releases, sales, free books, cover reveals and more.

Check out our complete list of authors, too!

No spam, no junk. That's a promise!

Sign Up Here

www.dragonbladepublishing.com

Dearest Reader;

Thank you for your support of a small press. At Dragonblade Publishing, we strive to bring you the highest quality Historical Romance from some of the best authors in the business. Without your support, there is no 'us', so we sincerely hope you adore these stories and find some new favorite authors along the way.

Happy Reading!

CEO, Dragonblade Publishing

Additional Dragonblade books by Author Rachel Ann Smith

Ladies of Risk Series
An Earl Unmasked (Book 1)
The Duke of Aces (Book 2)

PROLOGUE

Avondale House Party
Scotland

"I SUGGEST YOU cease glaring at everyone, or the moniker of Ice Queen shall transfer from me to you." Minerva, Isadora Malbury's oldest sister, harshly whispered behind her fan.

Dropping her gaze to the floor, Isadora replied, "There is not a single guest who we are acquainted with. Avondale's set are all strangers, and you know how uncomfortable that makes me." She covertly scanned the room once more. Her knowledge of the half dozen male guests was limited to what she could recall from *Debrett's*, which at present, meant she only knew of their titles and ages. Isadora knew even less of the female guests, who comprised of the gentlemen's sisters and ladies from neighboring estates.

Minerva's white-laced fan fluttered. "Which begs the question as to exactly how is it that we received an invitation."

Keeping her ties to the Wicked Ladies Salon a secret was extremely difficult, especially for Minerva, who was exceptionally perceptive. Isadora turned to her sister, who was at least acknowledging the other guests as they waltzed past them. "It was Lady Charlotte who extended the kind offer for us to attend."

"Lady Charlotte?" Minerva frowned. "She hasn't even been

presented at court." Her sister's frown deepened as she looked over Isadora's shoulder. "Our host has finally made an appearance."

Minerva need not have announced the man's appearance, for a surge of heat radiated down Isadora's spine, a unique sensation she experienced only when the man entered her sphere. Her natural abhorrence of strangers was oddly missing when the Duke of Avondale was in the same room as her. She stepped closer to Minerva as if her sister could somehow hide her from their host, which ignited a peculiar spark of interest within Isadora. A curiosity that burrowed under Isadora's skin and did not end until the man was no longer within sight.

"How strange." Minerva's gaze bored into Isadora. "It appears that the duke has decided not to grace us with his company this eve."

Isadora exhaled slowly. She forced the corner of her lips up and said, "Mayhap he simply wishes to be alone."

"Or it could be that the rumors he has his own agenda for the duration of the house party are true."

"What are you suggesting?"

"I overheard the matrons earlier. One theorized he has a paramour tucked away in his chambers, and the other believes he is on the hunt for a wife this Season and is assessing his options from afar."

Isadora's stomach clenched. "Both sound ridiculous to me." Isadora's mind and body began to react to the news, which should have neither bothered her nor intrigued her.

"I disagree. He is of the age where he needs to consider siring an heir. And since we know little of him and his set, his lack of appearance could very well be due to him choosing to remain abed with a willing woman. We both know someone who has that propensity."

"Aye. Father." Isadora's sire was an ungrateful and selfish man. The type of man Isadora swore she would never end up married to herself.

Minerva's sharp, intelligent gaze scanned the room once again. "There is a certain quality about the gentlemen that the Duke of Avondale chooses to consort with."

Mirroring her sister's actions, Isadora scanned the room to identify what it was that had Minerva on edge. Drawing upon her *Debrett's* knowledge, she rattled off, "An Earl. A Baron. A second son…they all appear to be gentlemen, nothing out of the ordinary."

"I wasn't referring to their rank. They are all shrouded with an air of danger. I can't help but think they are like foxes in a hen house."

"You have an overactive mind."

"So I've been told. Albeit three years of observing others from the fringes, I know one thing for certain—these men are not what they appear to be."

"If they are not idle, spoiled aristocratic men, what are they?"

"I've not formed an opinion as yet, but by the end of the house party, I hope to know if we should continue our acquaintance for the upcoming Season or not."

Isadora had a similar purpose. She was here on the behalf of the Wicked Ladies Salon to assess this year's applicant, Lady Charlotte, to determine if the lady was worthy of membership. "I shall do the same."

Minerva arched an eyebrow at her. It was obvious her sister was still concerned as to how they came to be guests among strangers.

"From afar, of course." Remaining aloof wasn't a problem for Isadora. Her gaze fell to a potted plant near the far corner. A shadow appeared and then disappeared. The Duke of Avondale? Isadora blinked. The dark form was gone.

What the blazes was her host up to?

Isadora shook her head. She needed to remain focused on her mission. It wasn't the Duke of Avondale who she needed to observe and deem worthy; it was his sister. Although the gentleman sparked a curiosity within Isadora. Inquisitiveness and a desire to solve mysteries were family traits she wished she didn't possess, but Isadora knew this oddity would haunt her until she fully investigated it.

She glanced at the laughing Lady Charlotte playing hostess. She was mature well beyond her mere eighteen years. Should Lady Charlotte be welcomed into the sisterhood of the Wicked Ladies? The only way to discover the answer was to spend the next two weeks at her host's side. Investigating the peculiar feeling His Grace evoked within her would have to wait until they were in London for the Season.

"I believe we've stood near the wall long enough." Minerva looped her arm through Isadora's. "Let's retire for the night and resume our efforts in the morn. I have a feeling that the next two weeks shall prove rather interesting for the both of us."

Isadora peered back over her shoulder at the ballroom full of guests. Minerva was correct. There was a shroud of mystery that enveloped the group behind her. As they made their way to their chambers, a premonition formed in Isadora's mind. The upcoming Season would most likely prove to be both entertaining and enlightening, but she wasn't sure for whom—her or Minerva?

CHAPTER ONE

Three months later…
London

THE CLINK OF glass brought Lady Isadora Malbury back to the present. Lady Sutherland's drawing room was filled wall to wall with unmarried ladies, all dressed in richly colored silk gowns. No boring white or ghastly pastels tonight. The energy in the room blazed along with the fire. No tittering behind fans for the Wicked Ladies this eve. No, her friends were all eager as she was to embark on another Season unwed and with the promise of adventure.

Isadora raised her glass filled with red wine, none of the watered-down variety served at meals. "To another spectacular Season."

The members of the Wicked Ladies Salon who had managed to convince their families to travel back to London early for the Season raised their glasses and repeated the toast with broad grins. The clink of crystal ensued, which was then quickly followed by chatter. Lord Sutherland's staff were kept busy refilling glasses and offering an assortment of mini hors d'oeuvres on napkins.

Lady Katherine, Countess of Sutherland, creator of the Salon, rested a hand on the barely visible curve of her belly. "Izzy, I shall be returning to the country shortly. The members have voted. You, my dear Lady Isadora Malbury, have been elected to champion the Salon and organize this Season's events. Do you accept?"

Isadora blinked twice and took another sip of her wine. What were the members thinking? This would be her second Season, and her debut had hardly been what one could call memorable. When not in the company of her fellow wicked ladies or surrounded by her siblings, the *ton* viewed her as nothing more than a wilting wallflower. She was the middle child, often overlooked, which had worked in Isadora's favor to date.

Isadora possessed no prior experience as a leader. She rolled the stem of her glass between her thumb and fingers. "Are you certain?"

She waited for Lady Katherine, who was five years Isadora's senior, to reply. The woman was a kindred spirit. They had instantly become fast friends upon being introduced a little over a year ago at the Royal Art exhibit, bonding over the advantages of blending into the masses. It was Katherine who championed Isadora's invitation to the group. The Wicked Ladies Salon was a haven for unwed women who dared to dream of—and participate in—adventure and vice.

One would never suspect these ladies that lined the walls at balls or occupied the shadowed corners, often referred to as spinster row, had formed a clandestine alliance and met monthly to escape their gilded cages. Members and former members were sworn to secrecy and to never publicly flaunt or discuss the existence of the Wicked Ladies Salon. The responsibility of maintaining the sanctity of the group now fell upon Isadora's shoulders.

Isadora scanned the room full of women who had shed their public personas at the front door of Lady Katherine's home. Regardless of if they were titled or not, wealthy or impoverished, each member was considered equal and seen as the intelligent and independent woman she was. Isadora mentally pledged to do her best. She wouldn't let her friends down. They had honored her with the role as their leader, and she would not disappoint them.

Raising her glass filled with water, Lady Katherine smiled broadly and said, "It was unanimous." In other words, Katherine had nominated her, and no one dared to defy their leader.

Isadora narrowed her gaze on her hostess and asked, "Of all the twenty members, some present, some not, why would you choose me?"

"Because Izzy, dear, you possess the restraint required to deal with all these members." No one but Katherine referred to her by the shortened version of her given name, not even her family. Katherine dug her elbow into Isadora's ribs. "Plus, I have every confidence that the power the position wields will not impede your decisions. I shall rest easy knowing that the Salon is in capable hands."

Capable? Isadora wasn't the capable one. That was Minerva, her eldest sister. She preferred to follow, not lead. Didn't she? Except, one of the reasons she had declared in her application to become a member of Wicked Ladies Salon was to step out of her sister's shadow and do something liberating and adventurous.

Isadora emptied her glass and held it out to an awaiting footman to refill. Glass three-quarters full again, she lifted it back in the air. "I shall endeavor to honor your wishes for the group." Isadora solemnly nodded. "My thanks for your trust and faith in me."

"I'm not worried in the least. I happily relinquish my membership and am glad it is you that will lead the ladies for the next phase of the group's growth. I'm proud of what we accomplished last year, and I'm a little envious I shall not be able to participate in this year's events." From the very beginning, Katherine had established the most important requirement for membership: the lady must be and remain unwed.

At the close of last Season, Katherine had relented and accepted Lord Sutherland's proposal, and they had wed over the summer. With the members of the Salon dispersed across the countryside, a vote to determine who was to succeed Katherine had been delayed until the majority could once again reconvene in London.

This would be her friend's last meeting with them, and Katherine blinked back the tears that threatened to spill over and asked, "Now tell me, will you be accepting the Duke of Avondale's sister's application?"

Squaring her shoulders, Isadora shared her concerns over the candidate for this year's membership. "I witnessed Lady Charlotte's keen wit and a remarkable ability for recall. However, her silent acquiescence to every demand made by her overbearing brother is rather worrisome."

What was more bothersome was the strong connection Isadora had witnessed between the duke and Lady Charlotte. The secrecy of the Salon was of utmost importance. Isadora herself had been challenged not to share with her brothers and sisters the exciting adventures she had partaken in last Season. She typically didn't hide anything from her siblings. Although Isadora suspected Minerva, the smartest person she knew, might have begun to piece together the snippets of gossip that occasionally hinted at the group's existence.

Complete anonymity with twenty members was extremely difficult to maintain. In the past, it had fallen to Katherine to select one individual to extend an offer of membership, and only after careful deliberation over the applicant's answers would she decide whether or not to officially grant them the honor of joining the Wicked Ladies Salon. The responsibility of deciding whether or not to formally accept Lady Charlotte's application and offer her membership now fell to Isadora.

Ill at the thought of having to question Katherine's motives and leadership, Isadora wrapped one arm about her middle. "Perhaps if you shared how exactly you came to select Lady Charlotte as a potential member, it might ease my worries."

"I confess, it was at my husband's recommendation that I

extended the offer to Lady Charlotte." Katherine avoided meeting her gaze.

Isadora asked, "And what does Lord Sutherland know of Lady Charlotte's character?"

"Sutherland is a close friend of Avondale's and views Charlotte like a little sister. He claims she is highly intelligent and fiercely independent. My husband fears if left to her own devices, Lady Charlotte shall seek out her own adventures, which we both know has the potential to be disastrous."

"Hmm." Isadora studied her friend's features. Katherine was a horrid liar. "Are you certain that Lord Sutherland is acting purely in Lady Charlotte's interest?"

Katherine's eyes widened. "Of course. If not for Lady Charlotte, who else would Sutherland be looking out for?"

"Mayhap the girl's brother. The Duke of Avondale."

"Many find it rather hard to say no to His Grace." Katherine rubbed her lower back. "I can't imagine why you would suggest that Avondale would wish for his sister to become involved with the Wicked Ladies Salon."

Her suspicion stemmed from pure conjecture. A belief formed solely based on the brief and few interactions she had had with the man while attending his summer house party.

Katherine's brows creased into a frown as she brought her hand to rest on her hip. It appeared to Isadora that pregnancy was rather uncomfortable—yet another sound reason not to wed. It was no wonder pregnant women were banished to the country-side, for if debutantes witnessed such discomfort, who in their right mind would willingly place themselves on the marriage mart?

Katherine sighed and, with dreamy eyes, said, "His Grace is rather dashing, and his moniker, the Duke of Aces, makes him sound rather intriguing. Sutherland says the man has Lady Luck sitting upon his shoulder, and only a gull would wager against the duke."

"His Grace is an overbearing peacock." Isadora placed her

empty glass upon the tray of a passing footman and turned to face Katherine. "My apologies. Peacocks are actually quite lovely creatures."

Katherine grinned. "Don't be shy. Go on...tell me what you really think of the man."

Trusting Katherine not to repeat a word to her new husband, Isadora continued. "His Grace was a most gracious host by refraining from making an appearance for the majority of the house party. However, when he deigned to join his guests, he exhibited an extremely high opinion of himself and was...was rather..."

Katherine chuckled. "Pompous. High-handed. Domineering..."

"Exactly!" Isadora sighed with relief. It was no surprise that Katherine fully comprehended. They often shared similar opinions on matters.

"I could go on and on, but since we are of the same mind, there is no need. It will not be without risk should you decide to grant Lady Charlotte membership. Now that she knows of our existence, there is also the risk of denying her application."

"And this is the quandary I find myself in. Do I trust Lady Charlotte to remain loyal to the Wicked Ladies Salon and uphold her oath to never tell, or will Avondale extract the truth from his sister and attempt to disband the group?" It was a conundrum that had Isadora lying awake many a night, thinking about His Grace and what he might do.

Yes, she had lost many hours of sleep pondering over the duke. She wished she could claim all her thoughts had been wholesome, except she couldn't. While she slept, her mind pictured him holding her close, waltzing with her at a ball, or embracing her and kissing her in a secluded alcove. Not that the man had even come within arm's length of her the entire duration of her stay at Avondale's country estate.

Katherine wrapped her in a hug. "Either way, I fully trust you shall make the correct decision." Her mentor released her and made her way toward the doors, signaling that it was time for everyone to disband and go home for the eve.

Why Katherine had placed so much faith in her, Isadora would never understand. But she had silently promised to do her best to ensure the members would have a wicked time this Season, and that it be remembered as one of the finest Seasons the women would ever partake in. She couldn't fail.

Her first challenge was to secure the location for their events. Wembly Hall had been home to the Wicked Ladies Salon meetings for years. It was perfectly located on the fringe of Mayfair, easily accessible and safe for the members to venture to unescorted. It would be ideal if she could continue to uphold tradition and continue to host their events at the worn but familiar location.

She made a mental note to seek out Mr. Wembley as soon as possible. She'd never met with a merchant before, let alone to discuss a lease for a building. Isadora's hand trembled with nerves and excitement. She was going to negotiate her first business transaction!

Marching toward the foyer, she smiled and bid her friends farewell. She needed to return home immediately, for there was much to do before the Season officially began in two weeks. It was going to be a Season of firsts. A Season she'd never forget.

CHAPTER TWO

S EATED ACROSS FROM Warren Dowling, the Viscount of Guernsey, his longtime friend from university, Thomas Grandstone, the Duke of Avondale swirled the light amber liquid in his tumbler. Previously, a round of cards at his friend's small but cozy study had lacked the same appeal as trouncing the man at a club. What had changed? He had, and it was all because of a woman.

Tom stared down at the swill that typically eased his mind and blinked. The image of Lady Isadora Malbury momentarily disappeared from his vision, only to return in a heartbeat. He had been a fool not to have noticed her last Season during her debut. Albeit he hadn't been on the hunt for a wife at the time. Regardless, as a seasoned spy, he should have noticed the stunning intelligence that shone in the lady's green eyes.

The two weeks Lady Isadora had resided under his roof this summer had been the truest test of his willpower. He had remained distant as he observed and assessed Lady Isadora's character, all the while combatting his increasing desire to discover what it would be like to have her close. He feared if he based his decision as to whom he should marry on pure physical attraction, he would be bound to a life of lies and deceit. He needed a woman who he could trust to keep his affiliation with the Foreign Office a secret.

Lady Isadora's cool, composed demeanor was refreshing. Not once did she bat her eyelashes at him or venture close enough for her to playfully swat his arm with her hand or her fan. No, Lady Isadora had firmly established her preference for distance, which would make her the ideal wife. He had deliberated for many hours over the need to marry this Season, and now that he had decided, there was only one woman who came to mind—her.

His natural desire for freedom and vice was tempered by the mere thought of the woman. His hope was he had not misjudged Lady Isadora and that she would prove to be the strong, resilient woman he had observed during her stay at his country estate. It would be imperative, for he led a complex and multifaceted life that required him to keep each aspect of his existence compartmentalized. His duties to the Crown must remain hidden from the masses. Upholding his family's reputation as being honorable, fair, and caring landowners was nonnegotiable. Partaking in the occasional card game and executing gentlemanly dares were a reward for his good behavior. But what of a wife? He would have to keep her, too, separate from his other activities.

Tom set his drink down on the polished wood table that was of the same light-warm brown tones as Lady Isadora's hair. Bah. It was pure fancifulness to liken the color of the furniture to a woman's tresses. He shook his head and picked up the cards Guernsey had dealt him and skillfully fanned the cards in one hand. Two aces and an array of face cards. Faro was a game of mathematical odds, not luck, which is exactly why Tom won the majority of hands. When required, he could exercise extreme patience and had a sharp mind for calculations. After arranging his hand to his liking, Tom set his hand back down and scanned Guernsey's study once more. There was a slight chill in the air despite the lack of square footage in the room and the fire roaring in the corner. He peered at the velvet curtains, but they remained unmoving. Something was amiss, but he couldn't pinpoint what it was.

Guernsey fell back into his chair and picked up his tumbler.

"While I was at White's earlier, I overheard a rather interesting tidbit."

Tom simply arched an eyebrow. He cared naught for gossip or idle chatter.

Guernsey emptied his glass and said, "Wembly Hall remains available to let for the Season."

Now that was interesting news.

Wembly Hall was a large venue, ideally located on the cusp of Mayfair. The hall could be used for any number of purposes, but for the past five years, it had been snatched up and sublet by the former bluestocking Lady Katherine. It had taken Tom nearly three years of investigation before he discovered who was responsible for securing the location for so long. Even after discovering Lady Katherine's identity, it remained a mystery as to what occurred inside the building.

Doormen who usually were easily persuaded to share information for coin were extremely loyal and refused sums that would have taken them years to have earned. Only those who were admitted were privy to the purpose for which Lady Katherine leased Wembly Hall, and that is what frustrated Tom the most. He had failed to identify any of the attendees year after year. He had a number of theories as to who and what occurred behind the closed doors of the place, but without evidence, that is all they were, mere suppositions.

Tom picked up his cards once more and shuffled them, taking one from the bottom and slipping it in between the others, over and over. The familiar movements brought about a calmness in him. "Mayhap Mr. Wembly would consider leasing the venue to me. We could hold our weekly card game."

Guernsey 's eyebrows shot up. "You want to lease Wembley Hall?"

"No need to look at me as if I've lost all my senses." Tom continued to shuffle his cards. The more he considered the idea, the more certain he was that it was a grand idea. Wembly Hall was the perfect space for him and his friends to partake in a little vice in private.

"The tightness of your jaw tells me you have already set your mind to the task. You shall have to be quick about things, for it is rumored Mr. Wembley is to meet with a lady early tomorrow morning."

"Does this lady have a name?"

"I believe it's the Ice Queen's unmarried sister." Guernsey studied his cards before him and continued to say, "The chit's name escapes me. She's rather quiet and…"

Before his friend could unintentionally make an offensive remark about the woman who had plagued Tom's thoughts, he supplied her name, "Lady Isadora Malbury."

"That's the chit!" Guernsey paused, rearranging the cards in his hand, and glanced up at Tom. "Not that I should be surprised by your excellent recall ability, but are you even acquainted with the young lady?"

"Charlotte invited the Malburys to attend our house party this past summer." Tom sighed as he confessed his errant sister's behavior. "My dear younger sibling extended the invitation without discussing it with me first." He had meant to press Charlotte for an explanation for her actions, but when he caught a glimpse of Lady Isadora descending from the travel coach, and their gazes locked, he quickly decided to let the matter go. Lady Isadora conducted herself with unparalleled poise, and when she caught him spying on her, Tom knew the woman instinctually possessed the skills of an agent.

Inhaling slowly to steady his suddenly racing heart, Tom reached for his drink and lifted it to his lips. The smooth aromatic brandy touched the tip of his tongue, and the image of Lady Isadora's gentle curves flashed front and center.

Women rarely caught his attention for more than a few minutes, and he rarely spent more than an hour or two with them in private. However, he hadn't managed to banish Lady Isadora from his mind after watching her carefully for the entire duration of her stay at Avondale.

He had caught Lady Isadora carefully observing the coming and goings of the house party guests numerous times and envied what appeared to be her innate ability to navigate through dinner each eve while seated between the most challenging members of the *ton*.

Yes, Lady Isadora Malbury met every demand on his long list of qualities that he had determined the next Duchess of Avondale must possess. Unintrusive. Self-reliant. Skilled at conversation. Intelligent. Poised. Quick-witted. Honorable. Confident. Observant. Amenable. It had taken two weeks for him to witness the full extent of Lady Isadora's skills. She had the ability to easily converse with others when necessary, but she also had the propensity to fade into the crowd undetected. While Lady Isadora appeared demure standing next to the other ladies, her eyes gave her away. She was full of life, ready to seek out adventure. She was simply in need of a guide. By the end of the house party, Tom had decided to seek the woman out this Season and court her.

Guernsey frowned and leaned forward to peer at his cards. "You must be mistaken. Sweet, innocent Charlotte wouldn't dare disobey you. She absolutely adores you. Everyone knows that."

"Trust me, I was as shocked as you to find out it was Charlotte who had extended the invitation to the Malbury sisters and their mama. However, I'm quickly coming to the realization she is not as sweet as one might think."

His sister was to debut this Season, and despite the fact she had proven to be one of the most effective agents for the Crown at the tender age of eighteen, Charlotte believed she had not yet reached her full potential.

"Why would Charlotte do such a thing?"

It was an excellent question. One Tom should already know the answer to but didn't. Frustrated at himself for having not taken the time to discover Charlotte's reasoning.

He squinted at his cards that were now clenched in his hand. "As you know, my sister has a mind of her own. I simply have to trust that she not only chooses her acquaintances wisely but also her future husband." Ready to end the evening early, Tom flipped over his pair of aces.

"Bloody hell, the Duke of Aces strikes again." Guernsey mucked his cards. "Mark my words, you shall need to keep a close eye on your sister this Season, or you'll certainly land yourself in hot water."

A shiver of fear ran down Tom's spine at the suggestion he meddle in Charlotte's affairs. If he interfered in her coming and goings, Charlotte wouldn't think twice about reciprocating the behavior. He didn't need his little sister meddling in his life. Tom rose and buttoned his waistcoat.

Prepared to take his leave, Tom said, "I should retire for the evening, given I'm to rise early to head off Mr. Wembly's meeting with Lady Isadora."

Guernsey stood and picked up both his and Tom's empty glasses. His friend trudged over to the sideboard. "Stay for one more drink. I wish to discuss one more matter that has been plaguing me for some time."

Tom had noted that the worry lines forged along Guernsey's forehead did appear slightly deeper in recent weeks. He sank back down into his seat. "Well, old chap, what has you foregoing sleep these days?"

Shoulders slightly slumped, his friend turned and sighed. "Over this past summer, I've been giving serious thought to the matter of my marital status. I've come to the conclusion I only have another five years before I become leg-shackled to some lady." Guernsey returned to the card table and held out Tom's refilled glass.

Tom accepted the beverage with a nod. "Five years, you say, why not ten?"

"While I'm not a master mathematician like you, Your Grace, I am capable of simple addition. In another five years, we will be a spry three-and-thirty. Another ten. Well, we might be a tad old to father a healthy heir. I've heard of men delaying too long and ended up not being able to..." Guernsey wagged his eyebrows and then continued, "You know...perform."

While Tom didn't disagree with his friend's logic, he fell into the old habit of playing the role of the devil's advocate. Raising his glass midway to his mouth, Tom paused. "Many a gentleman has sired an heir at the ripe old age of eight-and-thirty. You would not be the first nor the last to do so." His gaze remained steady on Guernsey to gauge his friend's response. When Guernsey didn't rise to the bait, Tom continued, "I'll confess, I, too, have given the matter of matrimony a great deal of thought this past summer."

"And?" Guernsey stared at him expectantly. "By Jove. The Duke of Avondale has decided to hunt for a wife this Season."

His friend was half correct. Tom had decided to go on the hunt, but he had already identified who his prey, no, his intended, was going to be—Lady Isadora Malbury. "Aye. I believe I'm ready." Declaring it out loud to another hadn't helped the mounting tension in his chest. Lady Isadora was perfect.

He had deliberated and determined that there was no logical reason for the lady to reject a marriage of convenience if properly presented to her. Lady Isadora had a fondness for risk. He simply needed to devise a sound argument as to why she should take a chance and trust him. That a marriage of convenience was what she was looking for.

"Bah. A man is never truly ready." Guernsey knocked back his drink. "No more talk. Let's play more cards."

Chapter Three

THE FAMILIAR WOODEN doors of Wembly Hall were within sight. Isadora's brows furrowed with each step she took, bringing her closer to the glorious location she had ventured to during the midnight hours over the course of the past two Seasons. Isadora scanned the building once more. It was nothing like the images she held in her memory. Wembly Hall appeared anything but majestic as the early rays of sunshine fell upon it. One of the many warnings Minerva touted every year floated through her mind—nothing and no one in Town is as exactly as they appear. Not that she ever doubted her sister's wisdom, but Isadora was disheartened at this newfound perspective on the place that had acted as a refuge for her.

She turned and glanced back over her shoulder at her maid to make sure she was there. She needed to secure the lease of Wembly Hall for the Wicked Ladies. She raised her gloved hand and rapped on the oversized door. The hinge rattled as her knuckles hit the solid surface. Repairs were necessary to ensure the safety of members. A wave of nausea hit her. She'd never been responsible for anyone other than herself, and now it was she who would be held accountable should any harm come to any of the ladies or if they were ever discovered.

No one answered. Mayhap she was early. Her hand shook as she reached for the latch and slowly pushed open the door to peer inside.

The hall was empty.

Isadora stepped through the threshold and halted. Hands clutched in front of her, she told herself, *I can do this. Even if my negotiating skills are not on par with Minerva's, I should be able to manage the simple task of renewing the lease for the Wicked Ladies Salon.*

"Are ye sure Mr. Wembly stated he wished to meet here?" her maid asked.

"Aye." Isadora pushed back her hood and scanned the space, picturing the smiling faces of the members of the salon. With a full Season of monthly events to plan, she sighed as she noted the deteriorating floors and cobwebs occupying every corner. She had her work cut out for her if she was to get this place ready in time for the first event. "What do you think of commencing the Season with a masquerade ball?"

"Isn't the masquerade usually scheduled as the finale for the Season?"

"It is, but I want the opening event to set the tone for the ladies." Isadora spun around in a circle and continued, "I want it to be a Season of daring, for this may very well be my last if Minerva has her way." The hem of her cape caught on a nail, halting her movement and returning Isadora's thoughts back to reality and the task at hand.

"Not if ye find yerself an understanding gentleman," Annie replied.

Isadora tugged the material free and sighed. "It is highly doubtful I shall attract the attention of someone as understanding as the Earl of Sutherland, who waited 'til the very end of the Season to become engaged to Katherine. The man even funded the second half of last Season's events, all because he wanted his intended to be happy." With a shake of her head, she continued, "The odds of finding another gentleman as kind and generous as Lord Sutherland are like finding a four-leaf clover in the middle of winter."

Her maid bobbed her head. "Well, if Lady Minerva truly intends for ye to be wed by the end of the Season, ye best make the first event one to remember."

Annie was right. The opening affair needed to be memorable, one she would never forget, one that all the members of the Wicked Ladies Salon would treasure. Booted steps and male voices floated through the curtains at the far end of the room.

"My thanks, Mr. Wembly, for agreeing to meet on such short notice." The familiar baritone had Isadora storming toward the stage.

What the devil was the Duke of Avondale doing here?

Mr. Wembly's chubby hand drew back the curtain. "Ah, Lady Isadora, I'm so glad you have arrived safely." The proprietor rose from a curt bow and motioned for her to join him as he waved his hand toward the side door. "Shall we all adjourn to my office?"

Ignoring the duke and the effect he was having upon her pulse, Isadora stepped forward. "Mr. Wembly, I do not care for surprises."

"Neither do I, Lady Isadora. Please, come join us." He walked over to the door and held it open for her.

Straight shoulders, chin held high, she waltzed past the Duke of Avondale, whose smug smile had her reconsidering if she should take her brother up on his offer to teach her how to box. It had been months since she had last seen the pompous gentleman, but her physical response to his presence had not changed. Her skin tingled and waves of heat rolled through her.

The duke followed close behind, his warm breath tickling the back of her neck, only intensifying her reaction.

Isadora took the seat in front of Mr. Wembly's desk, glad for her knees were suddenly weak. Once she was seated, the gentlemen slid into theirs.

Mr. Wembly's gaze darted between her and the Duke of Avondale. "As I was explaining to His Grace, Wembly Hall is in great demand this Season, due to the fire on the lower east side destroying both Astley's theatre and Cartman's hell. While we've received multiple offers for the rental of the space, my partners and I have decided to entertain offers only from the two of you."

"Why?" Isadora blurted.

Mr. Wembly's eyebrows shot up, then quickly formed a scowl. "Lady Isadora, it is…"

His Grace interrupted, "I, too, would care to know your reasoning."

Isadora's hand balled into a fist as Mr. Wembly smiled at her competition across the desk. "Well, Your Grace, collectively, we would prefer that the premises be utilized for…for more civilized pursuits."

Eyes narrowed, His Grace leaned forward, bracing his weight with one hand upon his knee. "Is that the case, Mr. Wembly? Or mayhap is it simply that your partners and you do not wish to invest in the repairs which both Astley and Cartman would demand of you."

Isadora couldn't help but turn her gaze to the man seated next to her. During the two weeks residing at Avondale, not once had the duke revealed this shrewd business acumen that he clearly possessed. His Grace had played the role of disinterested host and idle gentleman perfectly.

For what purpose did he wish to let out Wembly Hall?

In an attempt to settle her mind, Isadora returned her gaze to Mr. Wembly, whose cheeks were flushed, revealing they had indeed caught him lying.

"Please present the best offer you wish for us to consider." Mr. Wembly pushed a piece of blank parchment forward in front of Isadora and then another in front of the duke. "I understand you are both eager to have the matter settled. I shall consult my business partners this eve and will inform you of our decision on the morrow."

Tomorrow? And endure another day of uncertainty. No. She wanted the matter settled. Isadora focused her eyes on the man across from her. Mr. Wembly's forehead had a sheen of sweat, no doubt from the weight of His Grace's stare.

She shifted to perch upon the edge of her chair and leaned forward. "Mr. Wembly, might I remind you that my organization has had a long-established relationship with you, certainly..."

"Lady Isadora, I mean no offense, but without the personal backing of Lord Sutherland, I have concerns."

Gah. Men. The fathers, husbands, and brothers of many a lady controlled their funds. As with every standard, there were exceptions. Isadora knew of ladies who had managed to amass their own fortunes under pseudonyms. Pseudonyms like the ones Minerva had established for Isadora and their younger sister Diana. Skilled at calculating odds, she herself had amassed a rather tidy sum over the last two Seasons. One of the most highly attended events of the Season was the Wicked Ladies Gaming Night.

Isadora dropped her gaze to the blank parchment in front of her. Should she risk her entire savings to secure Wembly Hall? Minerva had specifically instructed her to only access the funds in an emergency. She was a full-grown woman at the age of twenty. It was time for her to make her own decisions. Volleying between wishing the sheet of parchment would burst into flames and seizing it, Isadora finally found her voice. "Very well, Mr. Wembly, I shall pen my offer in private and have it delivered to you by nightfall."

The Duke of Avondale unwound his long frame. "I shall do the same." Towering over Isadora, he proceeded to wing out his arm for her. "Please. Allow me the honor of escorting you home."

The gentlemanly gesture brought a frown to her brow. Normally, she would have to actively refrain from recoiling at the thought of touching another. Yet, her hand settled upon his sleeve as if it was the most natural action for her. An overwhelming sense of kinship invaded Isadora as he guided her toward Mr. Wembley's door.

She glanced up at the man that her body seemed to be instinctively in tune with. The corner of the duke's lips twitched. "The odds of being discovered with me are low compared to the probability of you finding a hack in time before you are outed."

His comment spurred the spark of irritation she needed to refocus. He was unfortunately correct again. Without the Season being in full swing, hailing down a hack at the crack of dawn had been rather difficult. The challenge of avoiding detection now that it was daylight would be even riskier. Isadora noted His Grace had modified his stride to match hers as if he was in no rush to be rid of her. She raised her gaze to him and inhaled sharply as his intense dark brown eyes bore into her as if he was trying to read her mind.

She removed her hand from his arm as he allowed her to step through the doorway unassisted. The sudden lack of warmth had her clasping her hand tightly under her cloak to prevent her from reaching out to touch him once more. She needed space between them, a moment to settle her rioting emotions that she was certain she was incapable of ever feeling before. She progressed through the main room, leaving Mr. Wembly and the duke behind.

Annie fell into step next to her. "What the devil happened? Ye've got color in yer cheeks." Her maid's gaze flicked to the duke.

"His Grace has offered to escort us back to Malbury town-house." She and her siblings never referred to the dwelling they were forced to reside in with their father as home. No, a home was filled with love and joy, neither of which existed at the townhouse. The constant chill that existed between her mama and father ensured that.

"How kind of His Grace," Annie said.

Mayhap accepting the duke's offer was the safest route, or was it? Caught traveling with the duke might raise questions.

Annie fell behind as the Duke of Avondale caught up to her in the center of the room. Isadora turned slightly to face the duke. "I accept your offer on one condition."

"And that is?"

In the short few moments away from the men, Isadora had managed to devise a plan. She shifted to include Mr. Wembly, who had joined them. "You shall make a sizable one-time donation to an organization of Lady Charlotte's choice."

"A charity of my sister's choice, is it? Pray share with me, what sum shall I be donating?"

She glanced at Mr. Wembly, who was broadly smiling like a cat who had cornered a mouse. "One hundred and fifty quid."

The duke's nostrils flared as he stared down at her. "Ridiculous. Absolutely not."

"Very well. I shall take my chances and secure a hack to transport me home." Isadora relied on her suspicion that the duke was much like her own older brother, Lord Kent. Benedict would never knowingly let a lady enter a public conveyance. She turned on her heels to take a step toward the front entrance.

Before her boot hit the wood floor, His Grace blurted, "Damn wicked woman. Stop. I shall make a single donation of eighty quid and not a penny more."

Isadora wanted to giggle at the duke's reference to her being wicked. He certainly made her want to be wicked, to test the man's self-control that was purported to be as strong as steel.

"I'm certain Lady Charlotte shall choose a most deserving cause." She winked at Mr. Wembly, goading His Grace.

The duke took one long stride to come to stand in front of her. "Be very careful, Lady Isadora. I don't foresee myself as being a gracious loser."

She stepped around the man, intending to continue on to the front door, ignoring the profound effect His Grace had on her.

From behind, he retorted, "I've not lost a single important battle—bidding on this building will be easy."

She whirled around to face him. All thoughts of propriety left her. She poked his chest. "Is securing Wembly Hall that important to you?" It was imperative she secured this place. She couldn't fail her first assignment as leader of the Wicked Ladies

Salon.

The Duke of Avondale took her hand and placed it upon his forearm. "I suspect it is as important to me as it is to you."

His touch once again muddled her mind, but she managed to go on. "Then it is extremely important."

SEATED OPPOSITE HIS prey, Tom cursed the gentlemanly sensibilities that had him inviting Lady Isadora's maid to ride inside the carriage rather than atop with his driver, all to prevent gossip. Hands clenched tightly in her lap, the young woman glared at him from the corner of the coach. She was obviously just as displeased as he was about the situation.

He wanted Lady Isadora alone. Verbally sparring with the woman moments ago ignited a desire within him that had nothing to do with his current physical discomfort and everything to do with his wish for a stimulating conversation. He hadn't even realized how deprived he had been of such a connection until today.

Streaks of sunlight streamed into the coach and fell upon Lady Isadora's cheek. Tom reached forward and jerked the coach curtains closed, blocking out the outside world. He wanted her for a wife, but not due to scandal. Shifting to lean back against the plush coach bench, Tom battled with his conflicting thoughts and emotions. It was a terrible idea to get this close to Lady Isadora and not be able to openly engage with her. He glanced at the lady's maid, who had wedged herself in the corner, and cautiously watched his every move. Tom shifted his gaze to Lady Isadora. He had called her a wicked woman out of frustration earlier, but the bright flare of interest that flickered in her gaze as she stared back at him unblinking had him wondering if his instincts were correct—how wicked could she be?

"Lady Isadora, I shall be frank, no matter the amount you

offer Mr. Wembly, I shall simply pay him double."

Her eyes widened briefly before she regained her composure. "That is rather magnanimous of you to inform me of your strategy to secure Wembly Hall. Although I had expected you to devise a more intricate approach since the Duke of Aces is known for both luck and skill."

"Is that so?" He crossed his legs, hoping to hide the bulge pressed against his falls.

"Aye. It's rumored that Lady Luck resides with you at all times, Your Grace. Mayhap we should test that theorem."

His blood heated as he sensed she was about to issue a challenge. "Go on."

"We have two weeks until the Season officially begins. Mr. Wembly stated he won't entertain offers from others. What if we came to an agreement?"

Yes, the woman was a risk-taker. He drummed his finger over his knee as if he was contemplating her words, when in fact, he simply needed to buy himself some time to adjust to the magnetic draw of the woman. "What type of agreement?"

Lady Isadora's maid chortled in the corner, reminding him they were not alone.

Ignoring her maid, Lady Isadora pierced him with her eyes. "A series of challenges." She shook her head decisively. "No, not challenges, three games of chance, and the winner shall gain Wembly Hall."

"Why limit it to three?" he asked.

"I'm not fond of wasting time. Wembly Hall is in the perfect location, yet we both know the building is in need of repairs prior to the Season commencing."

He admired her decisiveness and brilliance. "Valid point." He crossed his arms over his chest and tapped his forefinger against his upper arm as he contemplated her dare. "Are we discussing merely table games or other events that require Lady Luck to favor me?"

"Other events, such as?"

"Lord Derby is holding a race at Fulham tomorrow."

Lady Isadora nodded. "Very well. We shall each pick a horse to win. Whoever's horse places closest to first, shall be declared the winner of this round."

The woman was quick-witted and a delight to converse with. He had chosen wisely. Lady Isadora would make an exceptional Duchess of Avondale. There was still time to discuss his true plans, and Tom was in no rush to bring up the topic of marriage. He was enjoying getting to know his future wife. "Agreed."

The carriage swayed as they made a turn. Tom peeked out the window. Lady Isadora's home was a few blocks away.

Tom glanced at the maid in the corner and then, disregarding every rule he knew of etiquette, he leaned in and asked, "Shall we seal our bargain with a kiss?"

"Your Grace, your reputation precedes you. I, unlike the majority of my peers, have no interest in having your lips against mine. I'd rather kiss a pig."

Instead of offending him, the fiery, passionate response only made him hungrier to spend more time with her. "You misunderstood my intentions." He reached for her gloved hand, and when she didn't snap it back, he pressed a kiss to the back of her hand. The surprised look on her face was worth all the insults in the world. Knowing he was pushing his luck, he asked, "Will you grant me the pleasure of escorting you tomorrow?"

"On the condition that Minerva and Lady Charlotte join us."

It was his turn to be shocked. He hadn't expected her to agree. Arriving at a public event together along with family was nearly as effective as having the banns read at church—nearly. Before she could change her mind, Tom said, "I shall have it arranged. The invitation shall be on your family salver no later than this afternoon."

The coach rolled to a stop. He prayed his driver, trained to deliver him with discretion, had the foresight to stop in the back ally a few blocks away from the Malbury residence.

Lady Isadora's maid scooted forward and peered through the

carriage window before hopping out. With a curt nod, Lady Isadora followed her maid and slammed the door shut in his face. It was apparent the woman was quite independent. Another excellent quality to possess if she was to become his wife. Those that were faint of heart would not be well suited to the role of spouse to a Crown spy. Tom pulled back the curtain as the coach began to move once more. A chuckle rumbled in his chest as both Lady Isadora and her maid rounded the corner and marched up the path that led to her home. The pair proceeded as if nothing was amiss, and they were simply out for a stroll.

Tom reached beneath his seat and pulled out his collapsible writing desk. It was an item he had learned long ago never to travel without. Pen and parchment in hand, he drafted the invitation to attend the races within moments. Signing the missive in a flourish, Tom rapped on the ceiling of the coach to bring it to a halt. His loyal footman opened the door at the ready.

Tom handed the man the missive. "This needs to be delivered before Lady Isadora crosses the threshold of the Malbury residence."

His footman snatched the parchment and ran. The man was fleet of foot, and Tom sat back and grinned. Would the lady be impressed with his feat to have the invite delivered before she arrived home? He certainly hoped so. Tom rose and fell back into the space Lady Isadora had occupied on the forward-facing seat. The faint scent of lilac had him closing his eyes, allowing his imagination to picture the shock upon Lady Isadora's face.

CHAPTER FOUR

T HREE MORE STEPS.

Mr. Morton, the family butler, held open the front door with a sardonic arch of an eyebrow. He knew she was prolonging the inevitable.

Shivering slightly behind Isadora, Annie said, "Me hands are freezing, me lady. Let's stop dawdling and go in."

Her maid waited for a moment before giving Isadora a nudge in the back. The brief touch had Isadora's muscles tensing.

Annie shuffled her feet and whispered, "I apologize, me lady. May we please go in?"

Isadora wasn't ready to face her older sister. Not until she could banish the image of the Duke of Avondale's lips upon her gloved hand. She squeezed her hands together tightly behind her back, gaining some feeling in her own cold fingers before stepping inside.

Mr. Morton promptly closed the front door behind them. The butler took Isadora's outer garments and passed them to a footman nearby. "Lady Minerva requests your presence in the drawing room." With precise clipped movements, Mr. Morton stepped around her and led her down the hall to what she had no doubt would be an inquisition.

It wouldn't have gone unnoticed by Minerva or the staff that she and Annie had set off at dawn. Unlike her siblings, she enjoyed the whirl of the Season and loved being in Town, where the possibilities for adventure were endless. On Mr. Morton's heels, Isadora pondered over how she was going to hide the purpose of her early morning escapade from Minerva. Her sister knew her better than any other, and she was tenacious when solving the unknown. Thankfully, Minerva wasn't one to draw her own conclusions before asking for information first.

As Mr. Morton reached for the door, Isadora asked, "How long has my sister been waiting?"

Mr. Morton broke his own rules and gave her a lopsided smile. "Not long, mayhap a quarter-hour." He pushed open the door with his usual calm demeanor and announced, "Lady Isadora." What had prompted Mr. Morton's peculiar behavior? While unusual, it was also reassuring to find she wasn't the only one finding herself acting out of character.

"My thanks, Mr. Morton." Minerva's gaze focused behind Isadora. "Annie, please fetch us some tea."

Once the staff had scurried to do her sister's bidding and out of earshot, Minerva added, "And Isadora...you may close the door."

"What is it you wished to see me about?"

Minerva waved a bright white signature card in front of her. "I didn't push for an explanation as to how we received the invite to attend Avondale's house party, and I don't care to rehash the matter. However, I will demand you explain why we are to attend Lord Derby's race tomorrow."

Isadora frowned. How in the blazes had Avondale managed to have the invitation arrive before her? Gathering her wits, she met her sister's glare. "Lady Charlotte and I have become quite close. Mayhap the invitation was at the duke's sister's prompting."

"Why are you lying to me?" Minerva placed the parchment on the side table. "Sister, please come closer and share with me the truth this time."

"I can't."

"Why is that?" Her sister patted the empty space on the settee next to her. "Is it because you made a pledge that prevents you from sharing the truth with your own sister?"

Isadora walked over to the settee and sat. "You know?" Isadora shouldn't have been surprised. Minerva was extremely observant.

"Aye. I know all about the Wicked Ladies Salon." Minerva reached for Isadora's hand. "You can't be shocked. Did you really believe I'd simply overlook your covert disappearances over the past Season?"

Her sister's warm hand squeezed Isadora's, easing her guilt and nerves. Minerva was more mother than sister at times, and until today, had been the only person Isadora did not retreat from. Isadora dropped her gaze to their hands. "You never mentioned it or questioned me."

"It cost me a fair sum and a number of boons to gather the details necessary for me to piece it all together. And last Season, I spent a substantial portion of my pin money and the portion of your allowance that I'd managed to procure from you, on protecting your secret from other interested parties."

"What other interested parties? Who are you referring to?"

"None other than the Duke of Avondale."

"Avondale?"

"Yes, His Grace. Now, pray tell me what this…" Minerva reached for the invitation and waved it in front of Isadora, "is all about."

It was time to confess. Under Minerva's unwavering perceptive stare, Isadora exhaled and said, "Early this morn I set out for Wembly Hall to meet with Mr. Wembly to discuss the possibility of leasing his establishment on behalf of the Wicked Ladies Salon. However, it seems His Grace had similar intentions. When I discovered that the duke and I were both vying for the use of Wembly Hall, I proposed a wager of sorts. Best of three events or games of chance and the winner claims the use of Wembly Hall. His Grace agreed." Isadora nodded at the invitation still fluttering in Minerva's hand. "Tomorrow's horse race shall be the first of the three events."

Minerva tapped her chin with the corner of the parchment twice. Her sister was analyzing the situation. "Why are you responsible for securing the lease?"

"The members of the Wicked Ladies Salon voted me to be this year's champion."

Minerva leaned forward and wrapped Isadora in a hug. "Congratulations on your election. I'm extremely proud of you." Her sister gave the best hugs.

She hugged her sister back. "I'm terribly sorry I couldn't share with you about my membership with the Wicked Ladies Salon. I hope I didn't cause you too much worry."

"I shall always worry over my siblings, but I'm glad we no longer have to keep the existence of the Wicked Ladies Salon a secret." Minerva released Isadora and stood to pace in front of the settee.

Minerva turned her attention back to the invitation still in her hand. "While I know His Grace barely acknowledged our presence during our two-week stay at Avondale, others are not privy to such insight. Allowing His Grace to escort us to Fulham tomorrow may lead others to believe he intends to court you this Season."

Minerva was voicing her earlier thoughts and concerns. "The majority of the *ton* haven't descended upon London yet. I weighed the risks, and the race is nothing that will draw too much attention."

"That might very well be the case, but there are several influential members of the *ton* already present. Enough of them that should any impropriety be perceived...well...they will simply concoct their own version of the truth."

"Then we shall decline the Duke of Avondale's invitation and ask Gregory to escort us to the race," Minerva said.

Their brother rarely attended such events, preferring books and more scholarly pursuits.

"Would being courted by a duke be so terrible?" Her sister gazed at her.

"Considering there are but a handful of dukes in existence and only currently two unmarried—and one of those hasn't even reached his majority, and the other is a self-proclaimed bachelor, the answer is yes." Isadora bristled at her sister's smile. "Besides, I've not changed my stance on the subject. I shall not agree to a courtship until you are wed."

"Very well, let's not bother Gregory, and I shall send over our acceptance to Avondale House." Minerva's lack of questions didn't bode well. Her sister was scheming.

"I'm serious, Minerva. I shall not marry before you." It was the weakest of all her reasons not to wed, yet it was the one she was willing to admit to.

Most marriages amongst the peerage had nothing to do with love. She had endured a Season, which supplied ample evidence to support her theory that marriage was merely a way for men to transfer and gain wealth. She had other reasons for avoiding the parson's trap. One of which was to avoid a lonely union like the one her parents shared. Another was her abhorrence of physical contact.

Diana, their youngest sister, recently wed and now the Countess of Chestwick, confirmed Isadora's suspicions as to what occurred behind closed doors between a husband and wife. In her sister's latest letter, she offered rather vivid and enthusiastic descriptions of things that had Isadora's stomach in knots. An image of the Duke of Avondale's roguish smile flashed in her mind. Her breath caught. In the past, not a single gentleman had ever elicited anything more within Isadora than mild feelings of friendship. No fluttering butterflies within her. No rapid beating of her heart—nothing but platonic familiarity. Yet hadn't the Duke of Avondale made her pulse quicken? It couldn't have been because of the man himself.

No, her reaction was the result of his promise to take her to a horse race. Her love of horses and the lure of competition and risk is why she had experienced the heart fluttering. Isadora's shoulders slumped forward. She was a terrible liar, even when she was lying to herself.

"I anticipate this Season will be vastly different from those of previous years." Minerva stopped in front of Isadora, and her sister's sparkling blue eyes focused on her. "I shall see to it."

"I'm certain you will." Once her sister set her mind on a goal, Minerva was extremely difficult to deter.

"You would make a wonderful duchess."

"I heard that." Isadora groaned.

"Think upon it. Avondale is perfect for you. He is independent. Not twice your age…"

"You're wrong. Avondale is at least a decade older than I."

"His Grace is a mere nine years your senior."

Isadora stood and walked over to Minerva's desk to retrieve their latest copy of *Debrett's*. She found the page outlining the Duke of Avondale's lineage and sighed. "Blast. As usual, you are correct. But I know naught of Avondale." She snapped the book closed. "And what I do know of him is hardly what I consider worthy traits for a husband."

"Pray share. What do you know of Avondale?"

Did her sister suspect something or was she merely fishing for information?

Isadora returned to the settee and sank down to rattle off her limited knowledge of the man. "His Grace rarely dances or converses with unmarried ladies. He's a known reprobate. He flaunts his wealth and status to bend others to his will. You can't be serious when you state he is the ideal suitor for me."

"I do not jest. Avondale never acts without purpose." Minerva stood and sat at her desk and dipped her quill into the ink. "Tomorrow's outing shall be exciting."

The dark cloud that hovered over her sister the entire summer dissipated. Minerva's spark and appreciation for life were once again present. Isadora held her tongue and watched as Minerva penned their acceptance.

A heavy weight fell upon her shoulders. Was Minerva correct? By allowing Avondale to escort them to Fulham, was she about to seal her fate for the Season? For the rest of her life?

CHAPTER FIVE

SEATED COMFORTABLY IN the large ducal traveling coach, Tom's gaze remained steadfast on his sister as they made their way to the Malbury townhouse. He had pressed Charlotte for answers as they broke their fast this morning, only to find his sister's skill at evasion had not only improved but was highly effective. It had been a mistake to permit Charlotte to become involved with Foreign Office affairs. At the tender age of fifteen, Charlotte had caught the interest of the Head of the Foreign Office, who decided to train his sister. His own training had begun at the age of ten, and based on his knowledge of how precarious missions could become, he should have said no. Who was he fooling? No one denied the Head of the Foreign Office. Charlotte fidgeted with the row of pearls that adorned the edge of her kid gloves, bringing his thoughts back to the present.

With a grin, Charlotte said, "I can't believe you consented to take me to a horse race."

Tom inwardly groaned. He should have told her the full truth about his arrangement with Lady Isadora, but it had occurred to him over breakfast that, in the past few years, the two of them had spent less and less time in each other's company. He'd allowed his duties to the Crown to overshadow his responsibilities as brother and guardian. "Charlotte, I want us to be more open and honest with each other. I believe it imperative given our activities for the Crown. I'm forever at your disposal."

"Ahh. I understand." His sister's grin subsided into the barest of smiles.

Tom rubbed his aching forehead. "Actually, that's not possible, since I've not provided you with all the details." He took in a deep breath and then continued. "The truth is, Lady Isadora and I have entered into a wager of sorts to determine who shall have the honor of leasing Wembly Hall for the upcoming Season."

A wrinkle between Charlotte's brows appeared. She was too young to have developed worry lines, yet they were there. "Do you know for what purpose Lady Isadora intends to use Wembly Hall?"

"No." He leaned forward, resting his elbows on his knees. "But I suspect you do."

"And since you wish for us to cease having secrets, you believe I should share with you what I know."

"Exactly."

The twelve-year age difference between them had never presented a problem since Charlotte conducted herself with poise and grace well beyond her years. There was another woman that came to mind who exhibited those same qualities in spades, but he wasn't going to name her. No, he was going to exercise restraint. Damn it. Lady Isadora's image appeared in his mind no matter how much he tried to resist.

Scowling at his lack of mental control, Tom turned his attention back to the matter at hand. If he wanted Charlotte to share with him, he'd have to do the same. "I know that Lady Katherine has leased the location for the past several years. But what I haven't been able to identify is for what exact purpose. I suspect it was used for ladies to convene, but again, what goes on behind those doors has been extremely difficult to discover."

"Since my application has yet to be officially accepted, I suppose I'm not breaking an oath." His sister rolled her eyes. "Wembly Hall is the location where the members of the Wicked Ladies Salon assemble once a month to engage in various pursuits that could not otherwise be enjoyed."

"What do you mean your application has yet to be approved?"

"There are a number of prerequisites that a lady must meet in order to become a member of the Wicked Ladies Salon."

Tom waited for her to continue, and when Charlotte remained silent, he decided he needed to take a different approach. "Are you going to share the requirements or would you prefer I guess?"

His question brought back her smile. Charlotte sighed and unfolded her arms. "First, members must be and remain unwed. Second, members are admitted by invitation only."

"Was it Lady Isadora who extended you the invitation?"

"No. It was a dear and mutual friend of ours that saw to it that his wife extended the invitation to me."

"How can that be? You just said the members must remain unwed."

Charlotte arched an eyebrow.

Wicked Ladies Salon. Wembly Hall. Unwed ladies. Tom's mind raced to figure out how all the pieces of information he had fit together. "Aha. Lady Katherine." Lord Sutherland consulted for the Foreign Office on occasion and had recently wed over the summer.

Charlotte nodded. "Prior to Lady Isadora becoming the Salon's champion, the position was held by Lady Katherine. The Head of the Foreign Office believes it would be highly beneficial for me to become a member of the Wicked Ladies Salon, for a significant amount of information is shared behind the closed doors of Wembly Hall at their monthly meetings."

"Sutherland the crafty devil. It was Lady Katherine who's kept the man so well informed all these years."

"Brother, you mustn't let anyone know I have shared this with you. And especially not Lady Isadora, who is already suspicious of my reasons for wanting to join the Wicked Ladies Salon."

"Of course, I shan't jeopardize your mission. I could, however, assist."

Charlotte let out an unladylike snort. "How exactly do you believe you shall aid me in gaining membership?"

"Not gain but maintain your membership. I shall simply make it known to all that I wish for you to marry for love and only love. Given that our own parents' union was a love match, my declaration won't come as a shock."

"Is that what you are waiting for? To fall in love?"

"Absolutely not." It was Tom's turn to adopt the defensive pose of crossing his arms over his chest. "I have decided to wed this Season, and believe that the lady will agree with me that a marriage of convenience would suit."

Wide-eyed, Charlotte scooted forward. "Who do you intend to marry?" When he remained silent, his sister huffed and scooted back. "I see. You are only willing to trade secrets if it is to your benefit."

"That is not at all what I wish." Tom weighed his options. In order for his sister to trust him, he must, in turn, trust her. "I intend to court and wed Lady Isadora Malbury. If all goes according to plan, you shall be able to add matchmaking to your list of skills by the end of the Season.

"Lady Isadora? Have you gone mad?"

"I thought you would welcome the idea of Lady Isadora joining our family."

"The Malbury siblings are extremely close. They harbor no secrets amongst them. Why would you want to risk discovery?"

"That cannot be true, or do all the Malbury siblings know of the existence of the Wicked Ladies Salon?"

"Based on the information I've gathered, only Isadora and Lady Minerva are aware, and it wasn't Lady Isadora who divulged the existence of the Salon to her sister. I doubt there is anything that would prevent Lady Minerva from discovering the truth of any matter that she wishes to know. The lady possesses a keen mind and has exceptional skills at reasoning and deduction.

"Better than you?

"Aye, better than me." Charlotte clutched her hands in her lap. "As the sister of a duke, I am fortunate to gain invitations to the most sought-after events. As a bluestocking, I can maneuver with little interference. I can gain access and form alliances in groups that most overlook. As an agent of the Crown, I have access to resources other ladies do not have. And despite all the advantages I may have over Lady Minerva, she could outwit me any day. The woman is a genius." Charlotte peered out the window. "We shall arrive at the Malbury residence shortly."

Tom peered out the opposite coach window. He was proud of how diligent Charlotte was, always on the alert. "I wouldn't underestimate your skills or your abilities, Charlotte. You have risen quickly up the ranks and are now considered one of the best agents for the Crown by both the Head of the Foreign Office and your peers, which includes me."

Charlotte tapped his knee with the tip of her fan. "Before we collect the Malbury sisters, I wish to know..." She paused, searching for words.

"Yes, what is it you wish to know, sister?"

She inhaled deeply. "Out of all the eligible ladies, why have you chosen Lady Isadora to be the next Duchess of Avondale? Especially given you spoke no more than ten words to the woman during the entire two weeks she resided with us." Charlotte gave him the sweetest smile. The one that she knew he could never deny.

"I believe of all the ladies of my acquaintance, Lady Isadora is the most logical choice. She's well liked, even admired by some..." He pierced his sister with a knowing look, "and she has her own plans that shouldn't interfere with my own."

Charlotte's smile vanished, replaced with confusion. "You are the product of a love match, how could you wish for a marriage of convenience?"

"Love is not in the cards for me. Given the number of as-signments I'm given, I believe it would be best to marry a woman who is highly independent." He had stunned his sister into silence.

The coach rolled to a stop, and before the footman opened the door, Tom quickly said, "I shall trust you shall not disclose my intention to wed Lady Isadora until it is official."

"Of course, brother." Charlotte pinned him with a stare that had him frozen. "Likewise, I trust you will inform Lady Isadora of the risk she will be placing herself in should she agree to marry you."

"Papa never told Mama until after their vows."

Charlotte reached out, placing a hand on his arm, stalling him from leaving the carriage. "Mama loved Papa."

"Aha…so you will agree, love only complicates matters, best to enter a marriage of convenience."

Charlotte removed her hand and adjusted her skirts as she shuffled to the corner, making room for Lady Minerva and Lady Isadora. "All I ask of you, brother, is to promise to be honest with Lady Isadora and yourself."

Tom exited the coach and then turned around and popped his head back in. "I promise."

Charlotte raised her hand and swiped away the solitary tear which had escaped. "Go fetch the Malbury sisters, or we'll be late for the race."

As Tom turned to retrieve the ladies, the reality of his promise hit him hard. Was he being honest with himself? Was a marriage of convenience what he truly desired?

All thoughts and doubts fled his mind as Lady Isadora appeared. Her long strides had her dark blue, almost black, cloak gaping in the center, revealing a light pink dress. The woman's beauty had him forgetting to breathe.

"You're late," Lady Isadora said as she walked by him. Chin held high, she continued on to the coach.

Close on her heels, Lady Minerva winked at Tom as she, too, strode by and murmured a quick, "Your Grace."

He assisted the ladies up into the coach and then jumped in to occupy the rear-facing seat alone. Facing the three women, he decided it best to remain silent unless called upon for the remainder of the ride to Fulham.

CHAPTER SIX

F LANKED BY MINERVA on one side and Charlotte on the other, Isadora ignored His Grace, who was close behind them, and walked through the crowd of spectators whose energy was infectious. After the stifling coach ride to the race, she was glad to be outdoors. Fresh air, the scent of hay, and an array of pleasantly dressed men and women about lifted Isadora's spirits and nearly obliterated her worries as to what had prompted the Duke of Avondale to intently observe her as if she were a new specimen at the Royal Menagerie.

Isadora flickered her gaze between Minerva and Lady Charlotte, who were keenly scanning the crowd. A sense of calmness and security rolled through Isadora. She smiled at Lady Charlotte, who returned the gesture. A kinship of sisterhood that Isadora shared with all the members of the Wicked Ladies Salon was quickly forming with Lady Charlotte.

Minerva leaned closer and said, "You should approve Lady Charlotte's application."

Minerva's comment did not surprise Isadora. Her sister always had the uncanny ability to read her thoughts. "Why the endorsement?"

Her sister glanced over her shoulder, probably to check to see how close the Duke of Avondale remained. Apparently satisfied she wouldn't be overheard, Minerva answered. "She masks her extreme intelligence with precision and art that rarely occurs at her tender age of eighteen. Her vocabulary, riddled with double entendres, was highly entertaining. I'm certain you, too, would have noticed had you been paying attention to Lady Charlotte and not her brother during our hour-long journey."

The happiness that filled Isadora at being able to freely discuss matters with Minerva once more quickly dissipated at her sister's insinuation that she had been as preoccupied with the duke as he had been with her. "I heard every word Lady Charlotte uttered. Every word."

"Mayhap, however, you were not listening." Minerva linked her arm through Isadora's and brought her closer.

Her sister never acted without purpose. Isadora examined their surroundings, looking for Minerva's nemesis, Lord Mansville, or one of his cronies. She continued to search for a threat until she heard Lord Drake's familiar voice from behind, "Hey ho, is that Lady Minerva and Lady Isadora I spy?"

Drat. What was Drake doing here?

Lord Drake, neighbor and longtime best friend to her eldest brother.

Isadora twirled to shield Minerva from the man who had broken her sister's heart many a time over. "Drake, what a pleasant surprise." The man that Isadora had once hoped for as a brother wasn't due to arrive in Town for another two weeks. She should be beholden to Drake, for it was he that unintentionally had assisted Isadora to convince Minerva to leave for London early. Her sister had specifically rearranged their departure to ensure it didn't coincide with Drake's. Benedict. Blast—her eldest brother and his meddling ways. Benedict probably sent his best friend to keep a watch on them while he lingered in the country with his new bride.

The skin on the back of her neck prickled as Avondale took a step closer to stand next to her, fully barricading Drake from Minerva. "Lord Drake."

Instead of taking a half step away from the Duke of Avondale as she normally would, she fought the urge to sidle up to the man. Isadora held her position and glanced at Drake, then at His Grace. It wasn't simple recognition that flared between the two; there was a hint of defiance on Drake's part. What the blazes was going on here?

Her intuition screamed at her to pay closer attention to the duke than to her neighbor and lifelong friend. But every time Isadora focused on the Duke of Avondale, her mind went blank, and her body ached to get closer to him. It left her in a perpetual state of confusion, which she did not care for at all.

Drake finally nodded. "Your Grace." Drake's posture remained relaxed. "Isadora, I wasn't aware you and your sister intended to attend today's races." He presented His Grace and her with a semi-smirk that was his hallmark.

Before replying, Isadora glanced to her left to discover Avondale was openly frowning at Drake. Drake was well-liked by the majority of the *ton* and rarely garnered such a reaction. Avondale's frosty stare was quite refreshing, however not knowing what the reason was for the odd look between the two gentlemen, Isadora shifted her focus back to Drake and said, "His Grace extended an offer to escort us, and you know how much I love horses, we simply couldn't decline."

Tilting his head to the left to peer behind them, Drake's features transformed to mirror Avondale's. He was clearly displeased with whatever was going on behind Isadora. "Excuse me, it appears Lord Mansville and his cronies have arrived. I must go."

Isadora spun around to find that Minerva and Lady Charlotte were no longer in sight, and Mansville, her sister's tormentor, was indeed ambling through the crowd.

Avondale reached for Isadora's hand and threaded her arm through his and turned them toward the stables, away from Drake and the others. "Don't worry. Charlotte will ensure no harm will come to your sister, and if Drake is as capable as I hope, he should manage to dispatch Lord Mansville."

She wasn't as worried about Minerva at present as she was

about her body's reaction to His Grace's closeness. Isadora knew her sister was quite capable of defending herself. Minerva hadn't gained the moniker of Ice Queen without provocation. No, Isadora was more concerned at the curiosity coursing through her. Why did this man's touch make her body come to life rather than rebel? Unexpectedly, her fingers tightened about his arm. His muscled upper arm.

What were they discussing? Oh yes, their sisters. Refocused, Isadora asked, "Charlotte? Your sweet amenable sister?"

"Aye, and I can assure you she's not that sweet nor as biddable as everyone seems to believe." Avondale's lips curved into a smile that held the promise of secrets.

Secrets were every Malbury's Achilles heel.

She peered up at His Grace. Kind intelligent eyes. A straight nose that reminded her of the Elgin Marbles. And lips, lips that made her want to experience her first kiss. Heat flooded her cheeks. Why did her mind continue to stray?

Isadora returned her gaze to the stables a few yards in front of them. The familiar scent of hay and horses had her regaining her focus. If the Duke of Avondale was keeping secrets, she wanted to be the one to discover them.

His muscles flexed beneath her fingers. "Care to share what has you frowning?"

She couldn't tell him the truth, that her mind was preoccupied with thoughts of kisses and secrets, but perhaps it was an opportunity for her to gain some answers to a conundrum that had plagued her since the Avondale house party. "I was thinking upon Lord Drake."

"Do you share the same tendre for the man as your sister?"

The hard edge to Avondale's voice prevented Isadora from bursting out in laughter. "Good God, no. I was simply curious as to what you know of Lord Drake that made you refuse his plea to attend your house party this summer."

"I declined to honor Drake's request because your sister deserved a reprieve from all of her tormentors. She is extremely resilient, but after three Seasons, even the Ice Queen needs time to heal."

She shortened the length of her stride, and Avondale seamlessly adjusted without a misstep. It was as if he was in tune or had expected her reaction. Isadora didn't care for Minerva's moniker, but there was no changing it after three Seasons. Avondale's use of the horrid reference held a tinge of reverence when he spoke it, which meant he possessed a great deal of information about her family.

Curious to find out exactly what the man knew about them, Isadora turned slightly to face Avondale, giving in to the desire to observe his features. She was unprepared for the wave of warmth and well-being that enveloped her. Even in the presence of her overprotective brothers, she had never let her guard down. She was supposed to be attempting to lure him into sharing his secrets, not sharing her own.

Isadora halted, and Avondale did the same. "I understand denying Mansville and his lot, but Drake is a close family friend, not the enemy."

"Family friend or not, Drake is a stubborn ignoramus. I prefer the company of those who are intelligent and capable of sound logic." Avondale winked down at her.

Was he giving her a compliment?

Men didn't admire a woman for their brains. Avondale proved her theorem correct as he raked over her, inch by inch with his eyes. As if the man could strip her bear.

"We should find our sisters."

He released her and wrapped his arms behind him.

As if he read her mind, Avondale reached out to trace a gloved finger over the bridge of her nose. "Before we go, let us settle the terms for today's race."

Emboldened by Avondale's caress, Isadora teased, "You may be getting on in years, Your Grace, but you are not that old to have already forgotten that we agreed that whoever picks the horse to cross the finish line first wins."

Tom's serious demeanor remained. "I have not forgotten. But after further consideration, I wonder if you would consider a secondary wager."

"Beg pardon?" Isadora blinked twice.

"If I win, you shall agree to save me a dance tonight at Lowrington's ball. If you win, you may choose the next event to determine who shall gain Wembly Hall." He spoke with an urgency she didn't understand, but instinctively knew was important to answer him quickly.

"Agreed."

Avondale's grin beamed with admiration. "Impressive, no hesitation."

Avondale's smile had Isadora a quivering mess on the inside, yet she retained her exterior composure. "I've no concerns, for I shall win today. And when I do, I will have gained an advantage that will ultimately lead to me obtaining the one thing I truly want this Season. Wembly Hall."

The duke's smile briefly disappeared as if her response had wounded him. "I admire your determination to gain what it is you wish for." He winged his arm. "Shall we venture to the stables to make our choices?"

Isadora nodded and placed her hand on his forearm. "Yes, Your Grace, let's go select a winner."

CHAPTER SEVEN

TOM MARVELED AT the woman who walked next to him. Lady Isadora traversed with both purpose and elegance. She was also strikingly beautiful if one took the time to study her features—forest-green eyes lay beneath artfully shaped chestnut brown brows, ruby cheeks that were not artificially colored with face paint, and a gentle jawline that bespoke of power and confidence. At their every exchange, Lady Isadora reinforced his initial assessment that she was extremely capable and would always conduct herself with poise and grace, regardless of how challenging a situation she might find herself in.

Lady Isadora had an air about her that bespoke a single-mindedness as if nothing could sway her from a mission, not that he intended to train her to become an agent for the Crown. The Foreign Office had sufficient agents at its disposal in his opinion, which was not shared by the Head of the Foreign Office, who was recruiting more and more ladies to join their ranks. Charlotte's success and being the youngest female agent to ever be sent on missions without the aid of her handler only solidified their leader's views.

Tom suspected his sister's membership in the Wicked Ladies Salon was most likely part of the Head of the Foreign Office's new recruitment scheme, seeing as past efforts to recruit ladies to join the department had not yielded a high success rate. Should he heed Charlotte's advice and inform Lady Isadora of his involvement with the Crown prior to marriage? Many of his peers led double lives, choosing to never involve their wives.

He guided Lady Isadora through the wide entrance of the stables. The scent of horses and manure had Tom frowning as he recalled the details of his man of affairs report on the Malburys. His informants failed to discover any hidden scandals, at least none that she and her family had not already weathered.

In his experience, every family of the *ton* possessed at least two or three sordid secrets that could be bought for coin. The Malburys' had proved to be extremely skilled at hiding their secrets, but he wasn't one to be deterred. He'd gain Lady Isadora's trust and conduct an investigation into their affairs himself. It was crucial he knew of the lady's secrets if he was to marry the woman. The excursion today was devised to unravel her cool demeanor and reveal her secrets, however, his plan was failing remarkably.

Lady Isadora was in her element and appeared totally unaffected by his attention. He attributed her disinterest to her being a member of the Wicked Ladies Salon, given that the primary requirement for membership was to remain unwed. Blast and damnation. How had the existence and the activities of such a group remained hidden all these years?

He inhaled and glanced at the woman on his arm. His entire body relaxed, and his agitation dissipated like water on a hot plate. The more he discovered about Lady Isadora, the more intrigued he became. Her secret should be a deterrent, yet it had the opposite effect upon him. If he was to convince her to wed, he must first find out why she chose to become a member of the exclusive Salon. He needed more time with her. The idea of a secondary wager to gain him a dance at Lowrington's ball had stemmed from a primal wish to have her in his arms, but it would also prove to be a stroke of genius if he was able to simultaneously gain the information he needed to further his pursuit of Lady Isadora.

She dropped her hand from his arm and stepped closer to the horse pen. Her gaze was fixed on the prime horseflesh. "I shall back the Arabian to win."

Would she dare to reach out to stroke the beast? It would be highly unorthodox, yet exactly what he'd expect from a lady who was a member of a club named the Wicked Ladies. His gaze flickered from beast to woman. Lady Isadora's gloved fingers clamped about the wood railing, and to the untrained eye, might appear relaxed and enthralled with the horse before her. But the almost undetectable quick inhale of breath had him turning to face her. "Are you certain you wish to wager on this one?"

She turned and faced him directly. "Aye. He's a beauty."

Tom glanced at the horse, then promptly searched the rest of the stalls for a thoroughbred. None were within sight. However, as luck may have it, he did spy a slightly older quarter horse being brushed down and readied. "I shall place my wager on the old gray over there."

She stepped back to gain a better view. "Ah, he is a marvelous creature. It shall be a close race indeed." Lady Isadora scanned their surroundings.

With a few gentlemen lingering within sight, Lady Isadora's shoulders slumped. It was obvious she wished for privacy—but why?

"Come closer." Tom turned sideways, providing her with a shield. Her gaze lingered on the men milling about two stalls down. The moment he gave up hope she would acquiesce to his command, Lady Isadora folded her skirts, reducing her silhouette, and stepped up close to him. Her arm brushed against his chest and warmth radiated from the spot where she made contact with him. She had a peculiar effect upon him, which was hard to ignore. "Tell me what it is you want."

"I wish to ride him."

It was an innocent response from a well-bred lady. Yet, the breathiness of Lady Isadora's voice combined with the distinct longing tone of her response had Tom swallowing hard and banishing the image of Lady Isadora naked and straddling him in his bed. His days of being haunted by sexual fantasies were in the past. He was no longer driven by lust and carnal desires. His mind had mastered the art of control.

Tipping her chin up with his forefinger, Tom searched Lady Isadora's eyes. "If he should win the race, I shall have it arranged."

A devilish twinkle appeared in her eyes. She released her skirts and pressed both gloved hands flat against his chest. His skin burned beneath the layers of material that separated them. Lady Isadora lowered her right palm to cover his heart. She tapped her right forefinger to mimic the accelerated rate of his heartbeat. "You're not nervous that Lady Luck shall favor me instead of you today, are you?"

"Not in the least." His lips curled into a grin at her look of disbelief.

Here he believed he was the one in control of the situation, but the minx proved it was she who was in full control of the situation and him. His spine stiffened at the sound of footsteps from behind.

Lady Isadora took a large step backward. "Wait and see, Your Grace, the Arabian shall win, and I shall hold you to your promise."

THE THIN RAY of sunlight that peeked through the rafters bounced off the diamonds in Minerva's blonde coiffure. Her sister's arrival couldn't have been better timed in Isadora's opinion. Bending at the knees to remain in the duke's shadow, Isadora flipped open her fan and brought it up to mask her smile. Exhilarated at her newfound boldness and ability to touch another without her stomach revolting at the action, Isadora fluttered the fan in front of her. Verbally sparring with Avondale was entertaining but having the man's warm hard muscles flex beneath her palms sent a million sparks through her body. It was both terrifying and liberating all at the same time. Every encounter with the man unlocked another mystery her sisters had warned her about yet failed to explain.

Isadora peered around Avondale. Lady Charlotte waved while Minerva walked sedately next to the girl whose curls bounced like a spring on a carriage. The tension in Isadora's chest eased. Her sister's tormentors were not easily dispatched, yet both Minerva and Lady Charlotte appeared in good spirits.

"I believe I might have misjudged your sister," Isadora offered.

"Easy to do. She's a chameleon." Avondale turned to greet their returning party. "Sister, did you have fun exploring?"

Lady Charlotte nodded and peered up at her brother. "Indeed, I did." Despite the height difference, there was no doubt the pair were siblings. "I located a wonderful sweets vendor to the northwest."

Minerva's left eyebrow twitched. It was a signal the Malbury sisters used to communicate among themselves, indicating the speaker was lying.

Lady Charlotte looked up at her brother like he was a god. No one, not even the best actress on Dury Lane, could feign adoration like that. Avondale extended his arm for his sister, and they turned in unison toward the exit. The exchange had Isadora's concern about whether or not Lady Charlotte was capable of keeping a secret from her brother resurfacing. Isadora imagined it would be difficult for any woman to deny the Duke of Avondale the truth.

Isadora stepped up next to Minerva, who promptly elbowed her in the ribs. "I can't decipher their code, but their nonverbal cues are far superior to ours."

She watched the pair carefully, and they followed the Avondale siblings toward the exit. "Are you certain? All I see is a little sister fawning over her big brother."

"Have you ever once thought of looking at Benedict like that?"

Why would Minerva ask such a question? Isadora stared straight ahead and responded, "Of course not." Their eldest brother wasn't a charming duke. A man with dark mysterious eyes. Oh...Lady Charlotte was good, she mirrored emotions that others might wish to see disguising her true intentions and actions.

If Minerva was correct, then Isadora would have no fears in extending the one and only official invitation to Lady Charlotte to join the Wicked Ladies Salon. They invited only one new member to join their ranks each Season. On Lady Charlotte's application, she had stated her marital prospects were limited due to her overprotective brother. Observing the pair in front of her, Isadora suspected Lady Charlotte had only provided half the reason for her desire to remain unwed.

Minerva leaned closer. "I know that look, dear sister, and whatever suspicions you might be formulating, cease."

"You must be a little curious as to what Avondale and his sister might be discussing in code."

"No. My instincts tell me whatever the Avondales are involved in, it is dangerous. I was present when Lady Charlotte single-handedly outmatched Lord Mansville. You were not there to witness it. For three Seasons the vile man had me quaking in my slippers, and that lady..." Minerva pointed to Lady Charlotte. "She is no sweet young innocent, she brought Mansville to heel like a puppy on a leash—I'm still slightly in shock."

"Manville under a woman's control? Impossible."

"So I thought." Minerva smiled. "And yet Lady Charlotte accomplished the feat right before my own eyes. She is simultaneously remarkable and scary." Coming from Minerva, Isadora considered her sister's comment as rather high praise. No one scared or intimidated her sister, for it was normally Minerva who did the intimidating.

"Sister, dear, as you know, I have the sole responsibility of keeping the Wicked Ladies safe. Mayhap I should investigate more…before approving Lady Charlotte's application."

"Hmm…" Minerva searched Isadora's features. "Is it your intention to launch an investigation into Lady Charlotte or her brother?"

Isadora shrugged. Minerva might not admit it, but she loved solving a mystery as much as Isadora did.

CHAPTER EIGHT

TOM WALKED ALONGSIDE his sister as they followed the Malbury sisters through the crowd to the finish line. He wanted Isadora next to him, but first, he needed to speak to Charlotte. "I assume you were able to handle Mansville and his lot."

Charlotte's pleasant smile remained as she replied, "The dastardly man is persistent. His obsession with Lady Minerva is unwavering. Mansville will prove a challenge for yet another Season if Lord Drake doesn't come up to snuff."

"We are not to interfere unless Lady Minerva's life is placed in jeopardy."

"Why must we wait until a situation becomes dire? The man is an ogre."

Tom clenched his hands behind his back, not liking the orders handed down any more than his sister. It took him years to accept the rules. Regardless of whether he agreed with or found the parameters they were bound to abide by illogical, Tom followed them the same. "You ask this as if I'm able to provide you with the answer."

"Mansville may be titled and own a great many estates, but why the members of the *ton* and the Head of the Foreign Office continue to overlook his fiendish behavior toward Lady Minerva, I do not understand." Charlotte closed her eyes for a second and filled her lungs. After expelling a deep breath, his sister forced the corners of her lips back into a smile. "I apologize, brother."

They both nodded at a group of ladies as they tittered behind their fans.

Once out of earshot, Charlotte continued, "I have little confidence in Lord Drake after witnessing his behavior today. He remains within sight at all times, but he is also content to maintain his distance. Lady Minerva is acutely aware of his constant presence and directly advised me to ignore Lord Drake as she does. It wouldn't surprise me if Lady Minerva was devising a plan to flee from our social construct, but Mansville is cunning, and she won't be free of him unless…" Charlotte's gaze darted to her right. "Lady Sattersburg is here."

It was no surprise to see his former lover, Lady Abigail Sattersburg, on the arm of her new…older husband. Tom was fully aware that Abigail often bribed his staff for information on his whereabouts. "I wish for us to continue our discussion of Lady Minerva, but it will have to wait until after I've dealt with Abigail. Why don't you continue on without me."

Charlotte scowled at him, letting him know of her displeasure before quickening her pace to join the Malbury sisters.

His sister fell into step next to Lady Isadora, whose lips thinned into a straight line as she glanced at Charlotte's features. Immediately, Lady Isadora scanned the crowd. When her supple body stiffened, Tom suspected Lady Isadora had spotted Abigail approaching their party. He made it a practice to never dally with married women and had ended his affair with Abigail the eve of her wedding. Not that it appeared the woman marching toward him had accepted the fact that he was no longer interested, for the blazing desire in Abigail's eyes was evident to all.

Lady Isadora glanced over her shoulder at him with an overly bright smile. What the devil! Given her stiff posture, he had half-expected a glare of jealously, not a beaming smile that had his heart skipping a beat. The woman had him at sixes and sevens.

What was preventing him from declaring Lady Isadora as his

intended? No logical reason to delay except his instincts were screaming at him to slow down. He normally never ignored his intuition, yet the sudden urge to assert his claim was hard to dismiss. Lady Isadora turned her head away from him, and a chill descended over him. Tom disliked the frosty aloofness that was settling between them, but what was he to do?

He stood frozen, inundated by his rioting thoughts. The idea of marriage to Lady Isadora was quickly becoming a conundrum. He wanted a marriage of convenience. An uncomplicated arrangement that would fit in his already complex and convoluted life. He did not need to embroil himself in matters of the heart or enter into a marriage that might resemble his parents', which was proclaimed as an unparalleled love match by the *ton*. His gaze was once again trained on Lady Isadora's fine form. It was time he married. Every fiber of his body ached to be back within arm's length of Lady Isadora. With a nod, it was decided. Lady Isadora will be the next Duchess of Avondale. With his mind made up, why then did he remain rooted to the spot? The fear of rejection plunged ice through his veins.

He was no coward. Rather than heading off to deal with Abigail, Tom caught up to the trio of ladies. "Lady Isadora, a word please." If he intended to court the woman, he should start by dropping the honorific when thinking of her.

Isadora arched one brow. "As you wish, Your Grace."

He took two large steps away and waited for Lady Minerva and his sister to continue on in front. He was well aware that both wouldn't give it a second thought to eavesdrop if given the opportunity. As soon as their sisters were a safe distance ahead of them, Tom turned to Isadora and said, "I would like to alter our side wager for the race."

"I'm listening."

For the first time in a lady's presence, Tom's skill at charm seemed to evade him. "If I win, I gain the privilege of courting you this Season." He wanted to plant his palm flat against his forehead at his lack of finesse.

"Hmm… Why would you wish to raise the stakes to such levels?" Isadora glanced over Tom's shoulder. Who had Isadora spotted? Had it been Abigail?

Isadora turned back around and took a step back in the direction of the finish line. When he followed, she continued, "Some would say agreeing to be courted is akin to agreeing to marriage, and I assure you, Your Grace, I'm not on the hunt for a husband this Season."

Astonished at her rebuff, Tom asked, "Are you refusing my offer or worried the Arabian might not win?"

She scanned the strip of field where the horses were to race. "The course is longer than I originally estimated. A quarter horse of similar age to the Arabian would have a clear advantage, however taking into consideration your pick has a few extra years on him, I still believe it will be a fair race. What gives me pause is, I do not understand why you wish to increase the stakes, and what has occurred to prompt you to even consider such a preposterous wager?"

"The answers to your queries are simple. It's no secret I shall be turning thirty soon." He hoped he had masked the half-truth well enough for it to go undetected. Donning a look of what he hoped appeared to be resigned resolve, he continued, "It is time I wed…and after careful consideration, I believe you are more than capable of fulfilling all the duties of the Duchess of Avondale."

The back of her hand brushed lightly against his thigh as she clasped her hands behind her. "Your explanation is riddled with inaccuracies. First, unless my memory is faulty, you are currently only eight-and-twenty, which means you have at least another two years to search for a suitable wife. Second, we are mere acquaintances. You know nothing of me. Third, I can assure you, there is a litany of unwed ladies who are far more suited to become the Duchess of Avondale than me."

Isadora brushed her hand against him as she grasped her reticule. The minx was doing it on purpose. She glanced up at him, a twinkle of mischief in her green eyes, and softly said, "So your proposal to court me has nothing to do with your wish to gain Wembly Hall for the Season."

"Correct."

Clear disbelief shone through her gaze, and then in a flash, her eyes narrowed. It was mesmerizing to observe the woman next to him.

Isadora turned to look away from him. "Did seeing Lady Sattersburg prompt you to make such a hasty decision to wed?"

There was a hint of anxiety in her tone that hadn't been there before. "No."

Isadora's gaze flickered up to him. It wasn't a lie—Lady Sattersburg hadn't entered his thoughts in months. Yet he could tell by Isadora's shuttered gaze that she didn't believe his answer.

Horse hooves rattled the ground beneath them as footmen led the mounted jockeys along the rail toward the starting line. Tom rolled his neck from side to side, struggling with the urge to reach out and turn Isadora by the shoulders so he could see her face. The need to formulate a response of some sort to make the woman smile again and banish the anguish he had seen in her eyes moments ago was extremely uncharacteristic of him.

Lost in thought, Tom was startled when Isadora said, "Let's review the terms of our agreement before the race begins. Wembly Hall goes to the winner, best of three events."

Tom nodded. How easily Isadora had put aside her feelings and was now poised, ready to focus on the purpose of their outing. She was bloody brilliant in his opinion, and he was convinced there would be no one better to be by his side than Isadora.

Isadora's gaze continued to bore into him. "For today's race, if the quarter horse wins, I shall allow you to escort me to three events over the course of the Season. Should the Arabian win, we shall both attend Lady Thornston's soiree set for four days hence. She has a private parlor where we shall partake in a game of Rum."

Rum. The game was equal parts luck and skill like most card

games. His papa's voice echoed through his head, *Always bargain, never accept the first offer*. Six opportunities to convince her to marry should suffice.

"When my horse wins, you shall agree to six events, and henceforth you are to refer to me as Tom, and likewise, I shall call you Isadora."

She shook her head. "Four, and I'll agree to forgo formalities only in private."

"Agreed. Shall we join our sisters at the finish line? I wouldn't want there to be any mistake over who the winner is."

ISADORA PLACED HER hand upon Tom's arm, and the yearning to be closer to him eased. She had brazenly grazed her hand against him to test whether or not the ache she experienced would wane if she came into physical contact with the man. To her surprise, the brief touch had not quelled her ache but had also sent a jolt of delight through her.

Walking at a leisurely pace, Isadora took a moment to ponder the potential consequences of her wager with him. Tom was rumored to be a ruthless negotiator, and he was living up to his reputation. Courting. Marriage. No one sane would gamble on their future. Yet that was exactly what she was doing by agreeing to be seen with the Duke of Avondale, and especially so if the *ton* found out he was searching for a wife.

Isadora spied Minerva and Charlotte standing to the side. Her sister's gaze was flittering about the crowd. As she stepped up next to Minerva, she asked, "What's the matter?"

Minerva stepped forward. "We need to move faster. Drake is approaching."

"You never run from him. Why now?" Her sister's recent behavior around Drake had been extremely worrisome to Isadora. She wanted Minerva to gain the happiness she deserved, but Drake, the dolt, had still not attempted to win her sister's hand.

"He's going to attempt to ruin all my plans. I can feel it in my bones."

"And what exactly are these plans you speak of?"

"To have you happily wed by Season's end..." Minerva peered at her hand, settled upon Tom's arm. Tom was engaged in deep conversation with Charlotte and hopefully was paying Minerva's ramblings no mind.

Minerva wagged her eyebrows at Isadora. "To you know who."

Isadora released her hold on Tom. "You can't take credit for something you had no part in."

"Aha! You and the duke were discussing the possibility of marriage then."

Isadora shook her head. "I wish you couldn't read lips."

"But then I would be left out of so very many interesting conversations." Minerva's mouth curved into a grin that disappeared moments later.

Drake's familiar face appeared behind her sister. "What are you two lovely ladies fighting over now?"

"Drat," Minerva mumbled and then plastered a smile on her face but didn't turn to face the man Isadora knew her sister was still in love with.

Drake maneuvered his way to stand between them and frowned. He leaned in closer and whispered, "Isadora Malbury, step away from Avondale. You are entirely too close to the man."

How Minerva could predict Drake's actions with such precision astounded her. It was a shame Drake was too cowardly to act upon his own feelings for Minerva—they were perfect for one another.

Tom turned to join in the conversation as the sound of fingers snapping caught Isadora's attention. "Ah, Lord Drake, perfect timing. Might I suggest you see to Lady Minerva? I would hate for her brother, your best friend, Kent, to hear how you allowed those hyenas close to her." Tom raised his chin slightly to his left.

Isadora whipped her head about to discover Lord Mansville was yet again hovering nearby.

Drake swept his hand wide with a slight bow. "Minerva, Lady Charlotte, will you allow me the pleasure of escorting you the rest of the way to the finish line?"

Minerva and Lady Charlotte each nodded their consent. The trio moved forward.

Isadora was about to take a step to follow when Tom leaned in closer. "Nothing to fear. If Drake fails, my sister will prevail."

Tom guided her through the throng of onlookers, all vying for the perfect vantage point. She lost sight of Minerva. She could only hope that her sister would refrain from making any rash movements now that Drake was present.

Unable to assist her sister, Isadora faced Tom and asked the question that was top of her mind. "What alerted you to Mansville's presence?"

"Mansville has a particular habit of slapping his hand against the tails of his coat when he is in the vicinity of your sister. My sister has the hearing of a bat, a fact you should keep in mind at all times." He looped her arm through his as if he, too, wished to never break contact. "It was Charlotte who alerted me. Two snaps of her fingers alert me that there is danger close by. Three snaps is a request for assistance."

"What an intriguing system the two of you have devised."

"It's not our own, our parents taught it to us." A sadness washed over his features at the mention of his parents and then quickly disappeared.

Isadora recalled her father discussing with her mama—on one of the very rare evenings her parents both had sat at the dining table together—the tragic event of Tom's parents' death, lost at sea. She wanted to console Tom, but her sister Diana was the master of phrases, not her.

At a loss for the words to soothe, Isadora said, "Minerva also has impeccable hearing. I shall have to share with her of Mansville's habit, so she won't ever be caught off guard."

Tom effortlessly led her up a gentle slope until they were standing with a clear view of the finish line. "No need. Charlotte will see to it."

It was endearing how the Avondales treated Minerva like family.

Family? If she were to lose the wager today, not only would she be scrambling to win Wembly Hall, she'd also be fighting to retain her membership with the Wicked Ladies Salon. Isadora counted down the minutes until the horses were released and her future decided.

CHAPTER NINE

TOM NEARLY MISSED witnessing the quarter horse cross the finish line first. Isadora's expressive face had captured his full attention while the horses thundered toward them.

Eyes bright with excitement, Isadora turned to face him. "Well, my lord, it seems like Lady Luck continues to reside on your shoulder."

His pick had won by the barest of margins. "Perhaps. However, if the course had been a mere three lengths shorter, you, my lady, would have claimed victory."

"Are you always such a gracious winner?" She tilted her head slightly and narrowed her eyes upon him.

She was examining him like a bug under a magnifying glass, and oddly, he found it flattering rather than unpleasant. What did Isadora see? He hoped a man she could envision a life with. For every additional moment he spent with her, she proved his instincts were correct as usual.

From behind them, Charlotte said, "Tom's never so civil when he is the victor over me."

Isadora's gaze left him, and he wanted to curse the heavens for his sister's interruption. "Where is Minerva?" Isadora's finger bit into his arm as she searched the crowd for her sister.

"Unfortunately, after Lord Drake and I successfully convinced Lord Mansville and his lot to leave the races early for more lively activities back in Town, Minerva attempted to dispatch Lord Drake in a similar fashion and failed. At Lord Drake's refusal to leave, your sister stomped her foot, and it must have landed at an odd angle upon a rock because she let out a cry of pain. Before she crumpled to the ground, Lord Drake had her in his arms and pressed close to his chest." Charlotte looked at Tom. "He was quite the white knight carrying her all the way to his carriage."

"Minerva left with Drake? Alone? Did anyone else see them leave together?" Isadora's gaze fell steadily upon Charlotte, but concern had her voice wavering slightly.

The report Tom had received on the Malbury siblings expounded on their protective nature, but he hadn't fully understood its depths until witnessing it. His chest constricted. Without the danger and shared association with the Crown, would Charlotte and he be as close? He would have liked to think so, but perhaps their age difference would have proved a challenge.

Charlotte's eyebrows slanted down, forming a deep valley between her eyes. "I don't believe so. I apologize. The romantic gesture rather enraptured me." His sister's hands balled into fists at her sides.

As an agent of the Crown, they were trained to always be on alert and not be distracted. The weak smile his sister gave him was like a stab in the heart. Here he was fawning over Isadora, while he had sent Charlotte to deal with Mansville for a second time. Damnation. He should have taken care of the loathsome man himself.

Tom flickered his gaze between Charlotte and Isadora. "All is well. If Lord Drake and Minerva had set tongues wagging, we would have already heard whispers."

"Your Grace, I should like to return home," Isadora replied.

The combination of worry upon Isadora's features and Charlotte's sad eyes had Tom ready to depart post haste. He winged his free arm to his sister, who stepped up to slip her arm through his. He escorted the two women toward the rows of awaiting footmen at the ready.

Halfway to their destination, Tom bent to speak to Isadora. "I promise no harm shall befall Minerva."

"Your Grace, even you cannot make such guarantees. Minerva wishes to marry for love and for love alone. If it is discovered Minerva is alone with Drake, it will force them to marry, and it will all be my fault. I can't let that happen."

"Please, call me Tom." The insensitive request slipped from his mouth. He should be reassuring her not demanding more of the woman. "I can assure you, I have the resources to suppress any harmful gossip that might befall your sister."

"Why would you do that for Minerva?"

He glanced at Charlotte, who was doing a superb job of pretending not to be listening. Smiling and nodding at acquaintances as they passed, Tom turned his attention back to Isadora. "You have my promise. I'll never let anyone harm you or your family."

Isadora squeezed his arm. "Your Grace, you are avoiding the question."

"And you continue to ignore my request to address me by my given name."

"Very well. Tell me, Tom, why would you pledge such an oath to protect my family?"

He motioned for the ladies to proceed him and said, "Shall we postpone further discussion until we are comfortably seated in the carriage?"

Charlotte bobbed her head as consent, and Isadora's furrowed brow relaxed. "Agreed."

The women released him and stepped to the side. Tom approached the Avondale footman. "Have the coach brought around."

"Right away, Your Grace."

The footman dashed toward the long line of black lacquered vehicles. Having won the race and the wager, the duke should feel triumphant. Instead, he wished he'd lost merely to see Isadora happy again. Her shoulders were tense and the brightness in her eyes was replaced with worry. They waited in silence. Charlotte prompted him to say something, anything, but their code was limited to actions, not words of comfort. The ducal coach approached and stopped in front of them. Charlotte stepped forward to enter first.

Before Isadora followed, Tom reached out to brush the back of Isadora's hand that clasped her skirts tightly. "Is it Minerva's welfare that has you quiet as a mouse?"

"Partially. I know Minerva can manage Drake on her own." The faint lines about Isadora's eyes and at the corners of her lips clearly indicated she was worried. What other matter was causing her such unhappiness?

At a loss for words, he scanned the area for prying eyes. With no one in sight, Tom stepped closer and wrapped her up in his arms. Eyes locked on each other, they simply breathed in and out. After a moment, she relaxed in his embrace and he asked, "What is it that's bothering you, pet?"

She leaned back to peer up at him. "I lost the wager." Her chin dipped back down, and she stared at his cravat. Barely louder than a whisper, she continued, "I wanted… I'd hoped… Oh, blast, what I'm trying to tell you is that I rarely find myself in this position, and apparently, I'm not a gracious loser. A dreadful knot has settled in my stomach, and the ache has me feeling nauseous."

He relaxed his hold on her. "How about we agree that the first of our four outings shall be to attend Lady Thornston's soiree?"

She surprised him by wrapping her arms around his waist and pressing her delightful form to him. "You are a most gracious winner."

Tom wrestled with his guilt. He wasn't really a gracious winner. He was merely ensuring his plan was moving forward. Escorting Isadora to the soiree would be deemed a declaration of his intent to court her, and once he trounced her at Rum, they could settle the matter of who would occupy Wembly Hall. His decision to grant her wish had nothing to do with his desire to make her happy. Nothing. Lies.

Tom released Isadora and took a step back, and immediately regretted the space he placed between them. Having her close to him was fast becoming an overwhelming necessity. He assisted Isadora up into the carriage and hopped in, taking the seat facing both his sister and the woman his heart was melting for.

How was he to keep his hands off Isadora for an entire Season? Six bloody months was a long time. His skin tingled at the memory of her body. Tom shifted in his seat, spreading his legs to twirl his hat between his knees, all in the hope Isadora didn't notice his precarious state of arousal.

Tom searched his memory for intel on his host for the game that may seal the fate of Wembly Hall. Drawing a blank he said, "I don't believe I've attended one of Lady Thornston's events in the past."

His comment drew his sister's attention. "That is because you've never received an invitation."

"Why would we not have received one in the past?" Tom asked.

Charlotte glanced at Isadora and then back at him. "It is an annual, private event."

His sister was being evasive. "We receive invitations to exclusive affairs all the time. It is one of many advantages of being a duke."

"Invitations are extended only to certain members of the *ton*." Charlotte glared at him.

"Lady Thornston couldn't possibly be a member of the Wicked Ladies Salon. She's been married for years. Isn't the requirement of the group that members were to remain unwed?" Tom blurted, and Charlotte's head sagged.

Isadora looked at Charlotte and then at him. "How do you know of the Wicked Ladies Salon?"

Tom returned her stare. "This is not the first year I've wished to lease Wembly Hall. However, it is the first time it hasn't been already snatched up by Lady Katherine, who is now married to one of my close friends, Lord Sutherland."

Isadora's eyes widened. He had surprised her.

"Lord Sutherland would never have betrayed Lady Katherine. So let me ask once more, how did you come to learn of the Wicked Ladies Salon?"

"I told him," Charlotte confessed and shifted in her seat to face Isadora directly. Hands clasped tightly in her lap, his sister continued, "I understand this places my application for membership in jeopardy, however, Avondales live by a creed, no secrets amongst family."

"The Malbury siblings share the same belief, and while I did not share the group's existence with my family members, my siblings still discovered my involvement with the Wicked Ladies Salon." Isadora reached for Charlotte's hand. "You would not have told your brother if you did not trust him. Your application is still under consideration."

Isadora was an understanding and compassionate leader. Qualities rarely exhibited by those that wielded power. Lady Katherine had chosen wisely when selecting her successor.

Charlotte squeezed Isadora's hand. "I'm sincerely honored for the opportunity, but no matter what the outcome, I'm a better person for having spent time with you."

Egad, his sister was good with words.

Isadora smiled and relaxed back against the coach seat. "A formal invitation from Lady Thornston should appear on your salver in a day or two." Isadora glanced at Charlotte. "My apologies, Charlotte, only one guest per member."

Charlotte always hid her disappointment well, and today was no exception. He often forgot how resilient and strong his sister was.

With a smile, Charlotte replied, "I completely understand. I shall simply hope to receive an invitation next year."

Charlotte had informed him that if she were to become a member of the Wicked Ladies Salon, she would be privy to critical intel that could assist them greatly in investigations. If all the ladies possessed similar dispositions to that of Charlotte and Isadora, he didn't doubt the group had access to a mass of information that would otherwise be extremely hard to discover.

Isadora clasped her hands and gave Charlotte a wink. "I intend to extend this Season's new member invitation as soon as I have secured the group's meeting location."

How ingenious of Isadora to diplomatically lay the delay at his feet.

Tom glanced out the coach window. They were no longer traveling through the countryside. London buildings lined both sides of the road. It wouldn't be long before they would reach Mayfair and the Malbury residence.

When would he see her next?

Tom cleared his throat and asked, "Will you save me a waltz at Lowrington's ball tonight?"

"Claiming another boon so soon?" Isadora faced him. Her smile was a mixture of mischief and glee. "If Minerva is hale enough to attend, I shall accompany her, and I'll gladly reserve a dance for you, Your Grace."

Damnation. Her continued refusal to call him by his given name, even in the privacy of his own coach was infuriating. Isadora had called Charlotte by her given name earlier, why not use his?

CHAPTER TEN

THE COLLAR OF Isadora's dress brushed against the sensitive skin of her neck. She would wager a month's worth of pin money that Tom's eyes remained on her through the coach window as she mounted the stairs to her parent's townhouse. With each step she took, she inhaled deeply, and only after a count of five did she exhale. Setting her emotions aside for a moment, Isadora focused on preparing herself to enter her home.

Eager to check on Minerva, yet simultaneously dreading the series of questions her sister would have at the ready, Isadora assembled her thoughts that seemed to have scattered the moment the duke had suggested a courtship. It was absurd for her to even consider the proposition for a multitude of reasons, including her recent appointment as leader of the Wicked Ladies Salon. Normally, she wouldn't think twice about sharing the news with Minerva, who would unquestionably assist her in muddling through her new and perplexing reactions to the duke. They would discuss the matter, mayhap even laugh over the preposterous idea, but a crippling ache settled deep in Isadora's chest at the thought of making light of becoming the Duchess of Avondale.

The front door swung open, and Mr. Morton's serious gaze confirmed she had run out of time to dawdle. "Lady Minerva requests you join her in her chambers."

"Her chambers?" Isadora hurried to strip off her gloves and cape and handed them over to Mr. Morton. "Has Gregory assessed her injuries?"

Mr. Morton shook his head and patted his free white-gloved hand over his heart.

Blast Drake to hell. If Drake wasn't prepared to do the honorable thing and challenge Minerva to a game of chess this Season, for her sister had a standing agreement that any man that beat her at the game would win her hand in marriage. Isadora would have to devise a way to protect Minerva from further heartache. Tom's image floated before her. To date, Minerva's only reprieve from Drake had been the time they had spent at Avondale. A two-week house party free of Drake and Mansville's presence, Isadora had witnessed glimpses of Minerva's former self, a lady full of energy and optimism. If she were to marry the duke, Minerva could come live with them and be free of her tormentors again. Could she sacrifice her freedoms for her sister?

Mr. Morton cleared his throat, pulling Isadora from her thoughts. She picked up her skirts and ran up the stairs. Minerva hated to be kept waiting.

Isadora pushed open her sister's door and halted.

Minerva paced about without the slightest limp. In addition, Minerva had changed out of her pale-yellow day dress and was garbed in a deep red gown that was still rather risqué for a lady three years out.

"Sister, mine, I was told you had suffered an injury." Isadora stepped through the threshold into Minerva's chambers and closed the door behind her.

Her sister continued to stride back and forth at the foot of her bed. "I'm perfectly hale as you can see." Minerva paused momentarily and asked, "What was the outcome of the race?"

"Tom… I mean His Grace won the wager." Blast. Isadora braced herself for Minerva's reprimand for referring to the duke with such familiarity.

It only took two steps, and Minerva was toe-to-toe with Isadora. Her sister rose slightly onto the balls of her feet so that they were eye-to-eye. It required all of her willpower not to lower her gaze or take a step back.

Minerva finally asked, "Has His Grace given you leave to call him by his given name?"

"He did."

Minerva's lips curved into a broad grin. "However, I've only given myself leave to do so in my head and well…with you…and only in private."

"And what were the stakes of today's event?"

Thankful it was an easy question, Isadora's shoulders relaxed. "Wembly Hall goes to the person who wins best of four events."

"And?" Minerva quit her pacing and tapped her foot, waiting for Isadora to continue.

"And what?" Isadora wasn't ready to share the side wager with Minerva. However, with just the two of them standing in the room, she struggled to withhold the information that played havoc with both her mind and her heart.

"I've given it more thought. Weighed the possibilities. His Grace is a renowned gambler. Now tell me, what else is at stake?" Minerva resumed tapping her foot as she waited for a reply.

There was no way to fool her sister. Minerva knew every single tell Isadora possessed. Isadora sighed. "A courtship of sorts." She stepped back and bumped into the foot of the bed. Giving into temptation, Isadora let herself flop onto the bed. "No need to lecture me. I know I shouldn't have agreed to the terms but…" She sat up and with a surge of courage as she confessed, "When Tom is close by, it's as if my mind goes blank and my body comes alive. It's what I suspect you encounter when Drake is close."

Her sister shook her head and pinned Isadora with a steely stare. "Pray explain what you mean by a courtship of sorts."

"The duke is to escort me to four events over the course of the Season. Of course, his singular attention will set tongues a-wagging." Isadora rolled back and looked up at the blue and gold canopy. "It may well fare in my favor. Many courtships do not result in marriage. Having the duke's attention may well dissuade other potential suitors."

Minerva's foot tapping ceased. Isadora waited for Minerva to begin her lecture on the risks of giving preference to the duke. When Minerva flopped onto the bed next to her, Isadora turned to see her sister place her hands behind her head.

Her sister sighed and closed her eyes. "Despite all the heart-ache the man has caused me, you are correct, all rational thoughts flee my mind when I'm within ten feet of Drake."

Isadora frowned at Minerva's profile. How extremely peculiar. Normally, once her sister dismissed a topic, it was not to be addressed again. Except, Minerva was lying next to her relaxed and sharing emotions Minerva never hinted at experiencing.

"I shall not enter a marriage like our parents, and neither shall you. The inequity of love only makes one bitter. Mama is living proof." Minerva brought her arms down and crossed them over her chest. "I'd rather be put on the self, die a spinster than enter a loveless marriage. As for you, sister, if His Grace sets your heart aflutter, why not discover if he might share such feelings?"

For once Isadora was one step ahead of her sister. "I discovered today, Tom's heart races every time we touch, his eyes darken when he stares at me, and his brow crinkles when I share my thoughts. He appreciates my intellect, and that's what makes me giddy the most."

Minerva turned to gaze at her. "Physical attraction is not the same as love."

"I know this." Thoughts of Tom made her restless. "Do you think it is possible for someone to grow to love another?"

"Is it a possibility…absolutely. Is it likely… no." Minerva sat up and asked, "Would you agree to marry the duke if during your four outings he exhibited signs he might learn to love you?"

Isadora sat up and slid off the bed, then walked over to the window to gain some space. She could sense her sister was formulating a plan. "Mayhap, however, I won't marry before you."

"Why?"

Since Minerva was being open, Isadora believed it only fair to do the same. "I fear if I marry first, you shall disappear. I have no proof of my theory nor an inkling of how you would achieve such a feat, but I believe it in my heart."

"Disappear? I'm no magician." Minerva paused for a heartbeat and then asked, "Do you know if the Duke of Avondale and his sister intend to make an appearance at the Lowrington's ball tonight?"

"Yes, Tom requested I save him a waltz." Isadora waited for Minerva to react and say something, and when she didn't, Isadora turned around to scan the room. The chamber was empty.

Minerva had left without a word or a sound. Drat.

She flew out of the room to search for her sister. Isadora needed to dissuade her sister from whatever scheme she had planned, for there was no stopping Minerva once a plan was set in motion.

CHAPTER ELEVEN

TOM TUGGED ON his coat sleeve behind his back for the hundredth time as he searched the modest-sized ballroom for Isadora. The Lowringtons were one of a growing number of families who chose to remain in London year-round. Although most families had claimed it to be by choice, Tom knew it was more often than not due to a lack of financial resources. The combination of poor crop production and high estate costs for the past five years had emptied many of the lords' coffers.

Having scanned the room for potential dangers and establishing an escape if needed, Tom set off weaving through the crowd in search of the woman that continued to plague his mind. There was no sign of either of the Malbury sisters. Lady Minerva's note had arrived late in the day, causing him to scramble in order to meet her demands to see to it that both Drake and Mansville would be denied entrance should they present themselves tonight if he wished to dance with Isadora. He had sent the confirmation note that all was arranged three hours ago. Where the devil were the Malbury sisters? The doors to the ball were to be closed shortly.

On his third turn of the room, Tom nodded and stopped to speak to his hosts. "Lord Lowrington. Lady Lowrington."

"Your Grace," Lord Lowrington greeted as his wife dipped into a low curtsey and echoed her husband's salutation.

She said, "I hope everything is to your liking."

"Aye, the ball is a smashing success." He scanned the crowd once more. Candlelight glittered off the diamonds weaved through Charlotte's dark hair, reminding him of his chaperone duties. "Pray excuse me, I believe I'm needed by the refreshments table." He took his leave, not waiting for a response from his hosts.

Several gentlemen crowded around his sister, who was holding court with ease. It was going to be a long Season. Making his way over to his sister, a swatch of blue silk caught his eye. Isadora, along with her sister and mother, were waiting by the door. His feet continued in the direction of Charlotte, but his eyes never left Isadora's beautiful form.

"You shall trip and break your neck if you are not careful." Charlotte appeared before him, grinning ear to ear. "Proceed with caution, brother, both Malbury sisters have a gleam in their eyes this eve. I wonder what the pair are scheming."

Only half-listening to his sister's natterings, he noted Charlotte had already dispensed her gaggle of admirers. Unable to wait a moment longer, he presented his arm to Charlotte and said, "Come, let's take a stroll."

His sister obediently placed her hand on his arm without retort, which was highly unusual and gave him pause. He glanced down at Charlotte. "We are in accord as to what the objective is for the evening, are we not?"

"We are." Charlotte lightly squeezed his arm. "I'm to entertain Minerva, and you are going to attempt to convince Isadora marriage to you is the solution to all her problems."

Tom's gaze narrowed as he detected the sarcasm in his sister's tone. "If you have an issue with the plan, say so now or hold your tongue."

"I've already told you Isadora deserves more than a promise of a roof over her head and a monthly stipend. She deserves a husband who will treasure her, who will never lie to her, to love her, to..."

"Bah. I should have instructed the staff to burn all those torrid fiction stories you hoard in your room." It was a threat he'd never act upon, but Charlotte was being stubborn, and it reduced him to empty threats.

"While I may not agree with your reasoning, I do whole heartily approve of your decision to marry Isadora, and thus, I shall endeavor to assist you in achieving your goal."

They were a few feet away from the Malbury sisters when Tom caught Drake's image in the reflection of the glass of the grand clock in the corner. What the devil!

He had paid good coin to ensure the man wouldn't come within six feet of Lowrington's residence.

Charlotte leaned in closer. "I see we have a problem. Which would you like me to tackle—the Malbury sisters or Lord Drake?"

"The Malburys. I'll deal with Drake."

He was about to take his leave when Charlotte gave his arm another squeeze. "You have to give the man his due. Not many would have even managed to circumvent your orders."

"Drake's been on the Crown's list of recruits for years. Every year he declines for one ridiculous reason or another." Tom's gaze narrowed on the man's reflection. How in the blazes had Drake managed to get this close?

Charlotte released his arm and took a step back. "I wouldn't be so hasty to refer to Minerva as ridiculous if I were you."

"Minerva?"

With a nod, Charlotte said, "Lord Drake is like Father. He cannot bear to be apart from the one he loves."

Tom vowed he'd never be like his father. He'd not marry for love. Love clouded men's minds and resulted in unwise decisions. Drake's foolish actions only reinforced Tom's beliefs. Tom shook his head. "If you are correct, then why doesn't he simply challenge the chit in a game of chess, defeat her, and be done?"

"Mayhap he's uncertain if he could defeat Minerva."

"The man is a born genius. He's always three steps ahead of everyone."

"Aye, you and I are privy to such information, however, he has established a very convincing disguise he must maintain for the *ton*." Charlotte's gaze flickered to the windows. "Off with you. You're running out of time if you wish to keep your promise to Minerva."

He turned to leave and found both Isadora and Minerva standing before him, peering at him with questions in their eyes. With no time to lose, he simply bowed a quick greeting and then excused himself. Isadora looked spectacular tonight, but he wouldn't gain the opportunity Minerva promised to coordinate if he didn't go deal with Drake first.

Standing in the shadows of the dark terrace, Tom stood frozen and leaned to his left to catch Drake's mutterings.

The man paced in front of the servants' entrance at the back of the house like a caged animal. "Damn Avondale to hell... Escorting Minerva to the races..." Drake punctuated each sentence with a sharp turn. "Bribing Lowrington's men...what next...a dance or two... I'll break his bloody arms if he touches Minerva." The man's chin slumped to his chest. "Why had she sent a note advising me to stay away this eve? Did she hope Avondale would issue a challenge?"

That was enlightening. Apparently, Minerva hadn't trusted him to see to the deed of ensuring Drake was refused, and since the man was standing a mere few feet from Tom, she had been correct.

Tom spoke from the shadows. "I have no intention of playing a game of chess for Lady Minerva's hand. Which would be futile, for the woman would trounce me."

Drake whirled about and narrowed his gaze, searching the darkness. "Avondale?"

Tom stepped forward. "How did you manage to evade detection?"

"Answer this first. Why was I denied access to tonight's festivities?"

"Lady Minerva requested it to be so." Tom ran his hand

through his hair in frustration that he had failed.

"For what reason?"

"Ha! What makes you believe Lady Minerva would share her reasoning with me?"

"Not once did I receive a response to any of my attempts to contact her the entire fortnight she spent at Avondale. When you are about, it is as if she forgets my very existence."

At the mention of his house party, Tom's mind wandered. Isadora's sunny disposition had made his latest house party more tolerable. Now that he considered it, mayhap he had already decided to court Isadora before returning to London. She had been on his mind daily, and the last two days had been the most enjoyable in years. Tom's heart raced. He needed to send Drake away post-haste and return to the ball in order to accomplish his mission, possibly the most important one he'd set out to do to date.

Tom ushered Drake to the side gate. "I can assure you, I personally have naught to do with Lady Minerva's plans." He released the iron latch and swung the door open. "If I were to hazard a guess based on my very limited knowledge of the woman, I would say Lady Minerva is gradually distancing herself from you to lessen the burden before she executes her ultimate plan."

Drake stepped through to the other side of the garden wall. "If not you, then who do you suppose she plans on marrying?"

"You fool, Lady Minerva has no plans to marry. Are you so blinded by your love for her you have lost all your senses?"

The man was indeed like his papa, determined to stay close even when his mama was frustrated or angry with him. He would never let himself fall in love and behave like a fool.

"Avondale, you are correct. You know nothing about Minera. She wants children—a brood of her own."

"Then the decision to forgo that wish must cause her extreme pain." Tom's thoughts once again shifted to Isadora. Did she want children? He tugged at his cravat and raked his hand through his hair. It was a fact that he needed an heir, but Tom hadn't seriously considered the matter of children.

Drake barked, "You're wrong. You have to be wrong."

Tom shrugged. "I rarely am." Tom closed the gate and crossed his arms over his chest, waiting for Drake to take his leave.

After a minute of staring at each other in silence, Drake finally left, uttering a string of curses that would have made a sailor blush. With the task completed, Tom marched back to the Lowrington ballroom, fully ready to claim his prize. A dance with Isadora.

THE KNOTS IN Isadora's stomach tightened. She tore her gaze from the terrace doors and scanned the room. Blast. How in the devil had Tom reappeared from thin air? She suspected he had left to go to meet a woman in the gardens. Tom's rumpled hair and loosened cravat confirmed her suspicions—he had been with a woman, but where? His Grace must be like her papa, easily distracted by a pretty face.

Tom aptly made his way through the crowd toward her, weaving his way through the crowd like a lion stalking its prey through tall grass.

Isadora turned to Charlotte and said, "I'm parched. Shall we adjourn to the refreshments table?"

Charlotte nodded in agreement. She had been eyeing the group of gentlemen posted by the corner since she had joined Isadora and her sister.

Minerva leaned closer and whispered, "There is no avoiding His Grace all night. You promised him a waltz."

She remembered Tom's words from earlier regarding Charlotte's hearing ability. "Exactly, one dance. No more."

Minerva sighed. "Very well, mayhap a glass of ratafia would

be good. Lead the way."

Isadora took a step forward, leaving Charlotte and Minerva to follow.

Gloved fingers brushed against the back of her arm. Isadora slowed her steps.

"Where are you going?" Tom asked from behind her.

She didn't dare turn. Her anger was still bubbling to the surface. "To the refreshments table."

"I shall accompany you."

The fission of heat intensified along her neck and spine. She glanced over her shoulder to find both Minerva and Charlotte walking away from them. "I see I've been abandoned."

"Don't be angry with your sister, I asked Minerva to grant me the opportunity to speak with you in private." Tom's silky tones caused more havoc with her thoughts.

"Whatever for?"

He stepped up close. "Please, ten minutes, no more."

It would take less than that to be caught and bound into a lifelong commitment if anyone about inferred impropriety. "Go on. What do you wish to tell me? No one is listening."

"No, but they are observing. Come, follow my lead."

He placed his hand on her elbow, and with light pressure, he guided her back into the throng of guests. She frowned, observing Tom ignore the nods and smiles of acquaintances as they walked by. Caught off guard, Tom drew her into an alcove she hadn't noticed. She blinked, letting her eyes adjust to the darkness that enveloped them. The thick, heavy curtains not only blocked out the candlelight but also muted the music on the other side.

Isadora snapped her arm away. "Is this where you conduct all your clandestine meetings?"

"Beg pardon?"

Bottling her frustration, she asked again, "Is this where you take all the ladies you wish a private moment with?"

Isadora froze as Tom's hand fell upon her hips. "Since I spotted the alcove mere moments ago, and there is only one woman I would want to lure here, the answer to your question is yes."

"Aha! You admit you were with another earlier."

"You're accusing me of being with another woman." Tom's hands fell away. "I was in the gardens, dealing with Drake."

"Drake?" Isadora dropped her head and came into contact with Tom's chest. "Oh… Minerva was right."

He shifted closer, close enough for her to see his handsome features. Tom wrapped his arm around her waist. "Let's forget about this for now. Have you given any consideration to the advantages of becoming the Duchess of Avondale?"

Duchess of Avondale. The title, the role, preoccupied her every thought all afternoon. The question of how things would be if she were a duchess repeated in her head. Regardless of her illogical response to His Grace, Isadora wasn't ready to consider the full implications of having lost their earlier wager. "Your Grace, you won a courtship, not my hand. And as we both know, not all courtships end in matrimony. Many a lady's heart is broken when gentlemen fail to utter the four words they had hoped to hear all Season."

"Shall I utter them to you now?" A very beguiling twinkle appeared in Tom's warm brown eyes. That had Isadora considering saying yes…but only for a moment.

"The Season hasn't even officially begun. You know nothing of me. Why not wait?"

Tom placed a finger under her chin and lifted her face until their gazes locked. "I'm not looking for a love match, and if you are amicable to a marriage of convenience…" Tom leaned in to whisper against her ear. "I would be forever grateful, for it would save my toes from being trodden upon by debutants."

Her lips curved unwillingly into a smile and then his words registered, and she tried to take a step back. "A marriage of convenience? With you?"

He released his hold on her, giving her the space she silently requested, but his gaze remained on her. "Shall I recite the advantages I've surmised go along with the title you would assume?"

To buy time, Isadora nodded, then remembering they were in the dark, added, "Pray do."

"As a duchess, you will have a generous monthly allowance at your disposal."

Isadora blurted the first question that came to mind. "Enough to cover the monthly lease of Wembly Hall?"

He grinned. "Mayhap."

Apparently, Tom did know a thing or two about her wants and desires. But logic caught up with her, and Isadora's shoulders rolled forward. "Having access to large sums of coin after I marry will do me no good. I shall no longer qualify to be a member of the Wicked Ladies Salon."

He slipped a finger between the curtains and parted them briefly. "I spotted Lady Thornston in attendance earlier. I'd wager she is not the only former Wicked Lady in attendance tonight. Life doesn't end for the Wicked Ladies after marriage, perhaps you could offer them more than a reunion once a Season."

The idea of forming an alliance with previous members of the Wicked Ladies who were now married had its merits. "Go on."

"As mistress of all the Avondale properties, you would have free reign to host as many events as you wished."

Isadora raised her hands to settle on his chest. "So, if I agree to marry you, I'd have the necessary resources to ensure a fun and exciting Season for the former members of the Wicked Ladies. No restrictions."

"Aye. And there are other benefits…" His gaze lowered to her lips. "Benefits only a married lady may enjoy." He dipped his head and pressed his lips to hers, gentle, then more demanding.

It was her first kiss.

It was thrilling.

It evoked within her a bond she'd never felt with a man.

He ran the tip of his tongue along her bottom lip, seeking entrance. Her heart, which was already racing, pumped harder. She parted her lips, and the rich flavors of aged brandy and a slight hint of mint burst upon her taste buds. It was wickedly delicious, and a half sigh escaped her. He awakened her in ways she never knew existed.

Tom placed a kiss on her the tip of her nose before he eased back, placing space between them. He was breathing hard.

He placed a hand over hers that remained on his chest. "Kissing is the first of many advantages a married woman can experience."

"Are the rest just as wonderful?"

"Woman, you are going to drive me to distraction. Now is neither the time nor the ideal location for this conversation." Tom briefly closed his eyes and straightened. "All I ask is that you promise to consider the idea of becoming the Duchess of Avondale."

"I promise." Her quick reply garnered another kiss from Tom, and this one set her toes curling in her slippers.

When his lips left hers, he released her and quickly peered through the curtains. "We must return to the ball."

Isadora busied herself righting her sleeves. Was Minera looking for her? How long had they been gone? It simultaneously felt like mere moments and an entire lifetime. Isadora shook her head. What was she thinking? If they were discovered, the scandal that could ensue would remove all choices. Benedict, her overprotective brother, would end his honeymoon early and insist they marry by special license rather than wait for the banns to be read. She would be the next Duchess of Avondale.

Isadora placed her hand in Tom's. "I trust you know how to escape undetected."

"I do." He gave her hand a squeeze and then proceeded to lead her out back into the brightly lit ballroom.

Charlotte and Minerva were only feet away as if they had been guarding them the entire time. As they came to stand next to their sisters, Tom released her hand and whispered, "Don't forget about your promise."

She gave him a discreet wink. "I won't."

Minerva looped her arm through Isadora's. "I believe it is time we take a turn. In private." She bobbed a quick curtsey, pulling Isadora into one as well. "Your Grace. Charlotte."

Whisked away by her sister, Isadora mutely followed, preoccupied with thoughts of Tom. She had much to consider. Would marrying Tom allow her more freedom as he suggested?

CHAPTER TWELVE

I T WASN'T THE sight of Isadora reentering the ballroom flanked by Charlotte and Lady Minera that caused Tom's heart to thunder. No, his entire body tensed at the sight of Lord and Lady Torrance waltzing through the crowd headed straight for him. The couple rarely left the country early unless required to do so. Even before his parents' demise, Lord Torrance, who was a decade and a half older than Tom, had been assigned as Tom's primary contact.

The head of the Foreign Office preferred to separate the role of mentor and trainer from the role of a parent, which had been a blessing for both Tom and Charlotte when they lost their parents five years past. The stern look upon Lord Torrance's features did not bode well. It was highly probable that the couple was here on Crown business. And since it appeared Tom was their target, it was also likely they were here to inform him of his next mission. If he were to be sent away to deal with a foreign affair, it would jeopardize his progress in securing Isadora's hand.

Isadora. He searched the far side of the room to gauge her progress. Charlotte's brow creased as she spotted the Marquess of Torrance, and oddly Lady Minerva mirrored his sister's concern at the sight of the older couple. Isadora, on the other hand, appeared calm and unaffected. The sight of her lips brought back the memory of their kiss.

The passionate kiss had Tom questioning what type of marriage he truly wished for. He replayed their interlude multiple times in his head as he awaited Isadora's return. The ache that had settled in the middle of his chest as soon as she had left his side was what alarmed Tom the most. Was he falling in love? Tom shuffled his feet and adjusted his stance, unable to remain still. The woman stirred his blood like no other.

From the corner of his eye, Tom noted that the marquess and his wife were making quick work of cutting a path to him. It appeared that they would reach him before he could whisk Isadora onto the dance floor. The trio of women, Charlotte, Isadora, and Lady Minerva, were currently waylaid by their host Lady Lowrington.

"A good eve to you, Your Grace." Lady Ethel Torrance bobbed a quick curtsey and promptly straightened to her full height, which couldn't have been more than five feet.

"Torrance. Lady Ethel. I was not informed you would be present this eve."

Torrance nodded. "Neither was I until a day ago."

The man whose skill at decoding was only matched by his counterpart at the Home Office, scanned their immediate surroundings once more. "There has been chatter across the channel that our leader believes warrants further investigation." Torrance abhorred social events and idle chatter. The man never minced words, believing it best to always get straight to the point.

Damn the head of the Foreign Office. Tom may outrank his superior in title but not in the chain of command. "Send over the details in the morn, and I'll arrange to leave within a fortnight."

Lady Ethel bristled and glared at him. "Do you think I would have agreed to leave the safety of the country and hauled my boys and baby girl all the way to London if this wasn't a matter of urgency?"

"Luv. I'm sure His Grace will make the appropriate arrangements, now that you have informed him of the importance that he leave immediately." Torrance's arm settled about his wife's waist, and he gave her a quick squeeze.

Public displays of affection by married couples were considered faux pas. How many times had his own parents garnered admonishing whispers for exhibiting their love for one another? Too many, in Tom's opinion. Without care of censorship, Lady Ethel wrapped an arm about Torrance. Together, they faced him. A couple united and...in love. His heart and stomach simultaneously flipped. He wanted a union, a marriage, a partnership like that of Lord and Lady Torrance.

Tom sighed as his conundrum hit him. He couldn't directly disobey orders, but he needed more time. He needed to devise a plausible excuse, and quickly.

Aha. Love was the key.

He would convince Torrance that he had fallen in love, and he wished to secure Isadora's hand prior to departing. Sizing up the couple before him, Tom suspected it would be the only reason the pair would agree to a delay.

"I have a personal matter I must attend to before I can take on the assignment." Tom's gaze flickered in Isadora's direction.

Lady Ethel followed his gaze and then said, "Pray do not tell me you intend to extend an offer to Lady Minerva."

"Of course not, I'm no fool. I simply need a few more days to convince Lady Isadora that she has captured both my attention and my heart."

Torrance's eyebrows rose. "Are you claiming you are in love?"

"Is that so hard to believe?"

It was Lady Ethel who answered. "You wish for us to believe Charlotte's attempt at matchmaking succeeded? It was Charlotte who extend the invitation to the Malbury sisters."

"Aye, it was." Tom smiled at his sister's clever ruse to conceal the real reason she had extended the invite.

It was Torrance's turn to question him again. "Are you telling us that Lady Isadora has altered your beliefs on love matches? Has the Duke of Aces really found a woman he couldn't resist?"

Tom forced himself to remain still as the couple searched his features. He hoped he had managed to mimic his papa's continuous adoration for his mama.

"Is it really that improbable?"

Torrance answered, "Aye, it is. And I for one, don't believe your claims."

"Let us observe, husband." Lady Ethel turned and peered up at her husband. "If by the end of the eve we remain unconvinced, we shall set him aboard the *Quarter Moon* at first light."

"And if I prove I'm utterly besotted?" Tom asked.

Lady Ethel's eyes brightened with delight. "We shall assist and have you and your new bride aboard the ship within the week."

Regretting his request, Tom's chest constricted. It wasn't the idea of marriage that had him in a panic. It was the thought of placing Isadora in danger. "Isadora will not be accompanying me."

"If it is a love match, how could you possibly consider being apart?" the marquess asked.

His mentor had a valid point. Apparently, acting upon pure instinct was not the best strategy, but Tom needed the Torrances' support in this. He needed to speak in terms an agent would understand. "Isadora has commitments here in London that she will wish to attend to. I wouldn't ask her to abandon her duties in Town to accompany me on a dangerous mission for the Crown."

"Hmm, placing her wishes before your own…" Torrance looked down at his wife. "It is an indication of love." The marquess grinned. "You have until midnight to convince us."

Damnation. He was no actor of the stage. How was he to convince the insightful pair he was indeed in love with Isadora? He hadn't planned to share with Isadora the exact nature of his duties to the Crown. Dukes were often sent to represent the Crown as dignitaries, and he had intended on leveraging the common knowledge to explain his often-lengthy trips abroad.

Charlotte and the Malbury sisters were close. He snapped his fingers three times. Isadora's gaze darted about. Blast, he had forgotten he'd shared his secret code with Isadora earlier. He turned to introduce Torrance and Lady Ethel, but neither were within sight. Lord Torrance was a barrel-chested individual who stood at over six feet. How he managed to disappear and blend into the crowd in a blink of an eye was a skill Tom wished he could master.

"Ah, there the three of you are," Tom said happily as the trio came to stand in front of him.

"It's nearly time for you to claim your boon, brother," Charlotte whispered as she settled herself to his left, looking out into the crowd.

Minerva engaged Isadora in conversation, and Charlotte seized the opportunity to ask, "What did Lord Torrance share with you?"

"I've been requested to cross the channel."

"When?"

"Post haste."

"But what about Isadora?"

"If by the stroke of midnight, I've convinced both Lady Ethel and Torrance I'm in love with the lady, she may remain here safe on home soil while I complete the mission."

Charlotte looked up at him with a frown. Her mouth opened to speak, but then she shook her head and snapped her mouth closed. His sister never kept her thoughts from him—why now?

The opening bars of the waltz filtered through his thoughts. He turned to Isadora. "I believe I've been remiss in claiming my boon."

Isadora smiled and placed her hand in his. "I was beginning to think you had forgotten."

The frisson of pleasure at her touch had him questioning—where would she be the safest?

Guiding her onto the dance floor, Isadora turned to face him, and the answer hit him square in the chest. The safest place would be always by his side. He drew in a breath as he came to understand his parents' decision to always venture together. With understanding came acceptance. But was he really in love with Isadora? Surely not.

He extended his arm, and she stepped in to take her position close to him. His hand on her waist, he felt whole.

"Are you going to inform me of what danger lurks close by so I may be prepared, or are you going to remain silent on the topic?"

"Are you acquainted with Lord and Lady Torrance?"

"I've not formally been introduced. However, at my mama's insistence, I have memorized all the pertinent details shared in *Debrett's* of all living titled gentlemen." Isadora's brows scrunched for a brief moment before she said, "Torrance. Holds both the title of marquess and an honorary title of viscount. His family seat is close to yours, near the English-Scottish border. He married Lady Ethel six years ago and has subsequently borne two heirs, twins, which occur frequently in her family, and most recently he and his wife have added another member to the family, a daughter." Isadora's lips tilted up to one side. "What is not disclosed in *Debrett's* is that Lord Torrance and Lady Ethel's union is a love match. They are rarely seen apart, and it is claimed he is a master of riddles while she has the patience of a saint."

"Where did you obtain that information?"

"Where do you suspect?"

"The Wicked Ladies are well informed."

"It is one of the reasons for Charlotte's application, is it not?"

"Did my sister share that detail with you?"

"No, but I've gathered enough intel together and spent suffi-cient time with you both to know that neither of you acts without purpose. I'm still formulating my hypothesis as to what exactly it is you are both involved in, but I'm quite certain neither of you leads the typical idle life of the titled gentry." Isadora smiled at a passing couple and then returned her attention back to him. "You still haven't shared what caused you to snap your fingers thrice. And I wouldn't believe you if you claimed it was

Lord and Lady Torrance who posed the threat. They appear to be a lovely couple."

He caught a glimpse of Lord and Lady Torrance gliding across the dance floor. They moved as if they were one unit. He returned his attention to Isadora. She was masking her concern rather well. He tightened his hold on her. "I'm not at liberty to share details."

She didn't respond. Instead, her brow furrowed and her lips thinned. Despite the serious nature of their conversation, he didn't have to preemptively move his feet in order to avoid his toes being trodden upon, and he wasn't counting down the bars of music until he could return his partner to an awaiting gaggle of women or matrons. He was having a grand time on the dance floor for once in his life. His full attention was on the woman in his arms. If he didn't know better, he could even fool himself into believing he was falling in love with Isadora.

Isadora lightly drummed her fingers on his shoulder. "Hypothetically speaking, if we were engaged to be married, would you be at liberty then to share what has Charlotte hovering close by and pinning Minerva to her side?"

"Engagements are rarely broken, but it has been known to happen, so the answer is no." Tom twirled her to avoid another couple who were making eyes at each other and not paying attention to their surroundings. He smiled at Isadora's wide-eyed reaction to his response. Clearly, the lady was not accustomed to being denied.

"What would it take for you to confide in me?" Isadora's cheeks turned bright pink.

"You know how Minerva looks at Drake whenever he is not looking?"

"Aye."

"You would have to look at me like that for the remainder of the waltz and give me your word you are amicable to becoming the Duchess of Avondale as soon as I could obtain a special license."

Isadora's eyes softened as she gazed up at him. The glee at having her look up at him with adoration was short-lived. He wanted her to look at him because she, too, was falling for him, not to gain a piece of intel.

Isadora leaned in closer as if she were his lover sharing an intimate secret. "That's a king's ransom, you demand."

"Mayhap, but a deal you are willing to consider…give me your word to marry me, and I'll give you what it is you seek."

It felt like an eternity before Isadora met his gaze and said, "Keep your secrets. I will discover them on my own, one way or another."

Damn the woman. The last notes of the waltz faded into the background, and he escorted them off the dance floor. He hadn't achieved the mission he set out for himself this eve. He hated the feeling of failure. But had he succeeded in buying himself more time with Lord Torrance?

Depositing Isadora in Charlotte's care, he went in search of the couple, who in essence, held his fate in their hands. After thirty frustrating minutes, Tom gave up. Lord Torrance and his wife were nowhere to be found, and it wasn't even midnight. The thought of boarding the *Quarter Moon* at first light had his chest tightening. It was dangerous to conduct a mission without a clear mind. And the thought of leaving Isadora with matters not yet settled was crushing his heart.

CHAPTER THIRTEEN

DRESSED IN HER brother's breeches and lawn shirt, Isadora lay beneath the covers in her bed and tucked her hands behind her head. It might be hours before the entire household retired for the night. Minerva was full of energy on their way home from the Lowrington's ball. Her sister seemed suddenly optimistic about the upcoming Season, and while Isadora's intuition screamed at her to pry into her sister's plans, she remained silent and focused on her own plans for the evening. She had to discover what was the cause of Tom and Charlotte's peculiar behavior after the short appearance of Lord and Lady Torrance at the ball. That and the craving to experience more of Tom's kisses.

She threw back the covers and slipped on her riding boots and her brother's old greatcoat and carefully made her way to her chamber door. Ear pressed to the hardwood, Isadora inhaled deeply, gathering her courage. It wasn't the first time she'd ventured into the night alone. While sneaking out to attend a Wicked Ladies Event was exhilarating, sneaking out and attempting to enter a gentleman's domain was entirely a different level of heart-racing anticipation. It was no wonder, Diana, her younger sister who was now the Countess of Chestwick, had snuck onto Lord Chestwick's grounds months ago.

Isadora cracked open the door and peered about the hall. With all the candles snuffed out, she let her eyes adjust to the darkness before creeping out and venturing down the back stairwell. She hoped Grant, her loyal footman, had her mare readied and was waiting for her at the end of the back alley behind the row of townhomes. She smiled as she closed the back door and crept along the path that was no longer worn from lack of use over the summer. Isadora hopped over the rock wall and was relieved to see the small glimmer of candlelight at the end of the ally. She took a step forward and froze. The slight breeze held a fragrance that had her scanning the area. Bergamot. The cologne worn by Tom had been infused with the citrus scent. The duke was close by.

Hoping she was right, she whispered into the dark, "Your Grace. Please come forward." Her breath caught in her chest as she waited. The silence continued, and she closed her eyes to see if it would sharpen her hearing. She inhaled deeply. The male scent seemed stronger. He was closer, yet she hadn't heard a sound. Where was he?

Isadora spun around as warm air tickled the back of her neck. Shock rolled through her as she came face-to-face with a familiar male figure, but it wasn't the duke. "Drake, you scared me. What the devil are you doing out here?"

"Tell me first, were you expecting Avondale, or did I simply foil your plans to meet him elsewhere?"

"Neither." She disliked how accurately Drake had guessed her plans. The fierceness in Drake's eyes that she had never before witnessed had her staring at the man she'd known all her life with a different perspective.

Drake took a half step back and scanned their surroundings. "Isadora, the truth."

"I was on my way to speak to Avondale."

She had her own questions she wanted answered, but Drake asked first, "What was so pressing it couldn't wait 'til tomorrow?"

"He's in danger. I want to assist."

Her response elicited a chuckle from Drake. "Avondale can handle himself. Please return to your bed."

"Not before you tell me why you are out here lurking about in our garden." Isadora stood firm and crossed her arms over her chest.

Drake let out a sigh of resignation. "I wasn't lurking."

She looked up and spied the flicker of a candle from a window on the very top level... the attic...above the servant quarters. "Is that Minerva up there?"

"Aye. She's planning something...something extremely complex. I can feel it in my bones, and whatever it is, it has me worried. One day, your sister is going to have to realize life is not a game of chess. People are not always what they appear to be, and we can't all be easily manipulated as Mansville."

"Why are you worried? For three years you've done nothing but hover close by, but you don't act. Why won't you ask her to marry...and don't tell me it is because gentlemen don't marry their best friend's sisters."

When Drake remained silent, looking up at the window, Isadora tugged on her coat lapel and marched toward her awaiting horse and footman.

"Isadora, where do you think you are going?"

"I'm off to talk to Avondale. You can stay here and...and do what you do best. Nothing."

Drake flinched at her words. "If my life were as simple as it appeared, I would have asked your sister to wed a long time ago." He rubbed the back of his neck. "And if you intend to continue to associate yourself with Avondale, your life will become far more complicated than anyone will ever know."

Isadora turned slowly. "What are you inferring?"

"I'm simply advising you to stay away from Avondale."

"Goodbye, Drake." Isadora strode away, her heart was pounding in time to her footfalls.

Drake surprised her by following her. "Isadora, please heed my advice."

She rounded on him. "Why should I listen to you?"

"You're right." Drake ran his hand through his already

mussed hair. "Until I get my own affairs in order, I shouldn't be advising on who you should or should not associate with."

Isadora turned and took the remaining few steps toward her mare. She accepted the reins from Grant. And instead of her footman stepping up to assist, Drake interweaved his fingers and bent low to give her a lift to mount. "Be careful. And please don't get caught, or you will be reciting your vows before week's end."

"No one will recognize me, and Greg will watch over me." She smiled down and urged her mount forward. She was going to discover what all the mystery was that surrounded Avondale, and no one was going to stop her.

THE AMBER LIQUID in Tom's glass failed to ease the tension in his shoulders. He should retire for the night, but the uncertainty regarding tomorrow's events had Tom pacing in front of the blazing fire in his study. He had returned home expecting orders awaiting him, instead, on his salver, sat an invitation to appear at Lord Torrance's townhouse at the stroke of ten in the morn. His thoughts volleyed from anger and frustration to relief and excitement at the prospect of spending one more day in Town with Isadora.

A tendril of alertness ran down his spine. He placed his glass on the mantel and crept to stand next to the door that was locked. When the latch was released, he flung the door open to find Isadora rolling to her feet from a crouched position. There hadn't been sufficient time for her to hide lock picks from sight, so how in tarnation had she picked the lock?

Eyes twinkling with mischief and lips curved into a wicked smile, Isadora peered up at him. "Good evening, Your Grace."

He gave her his hand, and she placed her gloved hand in his and rolled to her feet. He grinned at the woman, who continued to amaze him. "A good eve to you, Isadora." He stepped to the side and motioned for her to enter.

She strode across the room, stripped out of her cloak and gloves, placing them on the wingback chair next to the fire. "You are probably wondering why I'm here."

Her body shivered. Brandy would warm the woman from the inside out. Tom reached for his glass and moved to the sideboard to refill his and to pour Isadora a generous finger. Tumblers in hand, he joined her by the fire. "Drink?"

She accepted the glass and swirled the liquid about. "French." She lifted the glass and sniffed as if she were a connoisseur. "From the south and definitely smuggled." Without hesitation, she raised the glass and took a healthy sip.

Isadora was bold and full of surprises. Not many people caught Tom by surprise. He often prided himself on being able to foretell a person's actions, which in many instances had been the difference between life and death. When he was in his early twenties, he had volunteered for the most dangerous of missions to test his skills, but after inheriting the title and becoming Charlotte's guardian, he had refrained from venturing too far from home and accepting assignments that had the potential to end on dire terms. Until he produced an heir, he would continue to adhere to the self-imposed restrictions. An image of a little boy with green eyes appeared, and he found himself stepping closer to Isadora. "Ready to share why you are here?"

She took another sip before cupping her glass with both hands. "You believed you were in danger earlier tonight." Isadora redirected her gaze from the fire to him. "Don't deny you signaled to Charlotte for support. I heard you snap your fingers. If I'm to seriously consider the position of duchess, I need to know if by marrying you there is the potential of placing my family at risk."

"You are not concerned for your own welfare."

"I can take care of myself, but I shall not willingly place any of my siblings or their spouses in jeopardy."

Not surprised by her devotion, Tom replied, "Hypothetically, if I were to be an agent for the Crown, would you consider my proposal?"

"I knew it!" Isadora's gorgeous green eyes came alive. "I knew you were a spy." She placed her glass on the mantel and twirled on the ball of her foot to face him. "That is why you wish for a marriage of convenience. It's the reason that you've chosen to marry me, well, I mean to marry someone who has her own secrets to keep."

It wasn't his reasoning, but Tom marveled at the woman's logic, nonetheless. "Then you will marry me?"

"Understanding your motivations does assist me in making my decision, however, I need more time."

With his departure looming, he was no longer willing to debate the issue. "We are running out of time." He reached for her and wrapped his arms around her waist, bringing her closer until she had to tilt her head back to see him. For once, he didn't analyze the situation, he simply acted, lowering his mouth to hers.

Alone in his study, he had the privacy necessary to show her some of the wicked benefits she could expect if she agreed to wed. Isadora was a quick study, and it was she who teased his mouth open to deepen the kiss. Her bold actions heightened his response. The desperate need to taste more of her, share more of him than he ever dared to before, had Tom sliding his hands lower to her hips. Isadora responded enthusiastically, pressing closer. His palms shifted to cup her bottom, urging her to wrap her legs about him.

With her arms linked around his neck, Isadora complied with his silent request. He carried her across the room and sat her on the edge of his desk. The friction against his erect cock had him yearning to be wedged between her thighs and sheathing himself to the hilt. But she was an innocent, and he would not take her maidenhood before they wed. He had no restraint over his reaction to Isadora's mewls of pleasure.

Tom nuzzled her neck and mumbled close to her ear, "I want

to touch you." She tilted her head, exposing more of her soft skin. Tempting him. He ran his tongue along the long column of her neck while he simultaneously reached for her breeches. He reached beneath the material and glided his hand over her stomach and down until his fingers brushed against the soft curls that protected the sensitive mound he sought to touch. She peered up at him, her gaze trained on his lips. Her eyes glittered with desire and…and trust.

She trusted him. He would give her a glimpse into what being married to him would offer, but refrain from fully compromising her. He didn't want to make the choice for her.

He bent at the knees and brushed his mouth over hers, not once but twice until she opened for him. He made quick work of opening her breeches and pulling them down to her ankles. As if his fingers had a mind of their own, his forefinger trailed down her womanhood and a groan escaped him as his finger slid deeper between her folds.

Rolling her hips forward, Isadora pressed against his palm, and he slowly inched his finger inside of her and then retracted it. His manhood pulsed with desire. Ignoring his own needs, he repeated the motion, drawing a guttural moan from Isadora. She skimmed her hand down his chest and continued lower below his waistband until she could cup his erection. He was certain she had no idea what she was doing, but she trusted her instincts and him. He continued to plunge a finger in and out of her and delighted in how she arched her back and cried out for more. The delight on her face washed through him. It was an encounter he'd never experienced but wanted to again and again. And as she reached her peak, he admired the pretty pink flush that suffused her body. It was a vision to behold. Something he'd never forget.

While he still had enough self-control, he withdrew his hand, trailing the back of his hand along her inner thigh, remaining in contact with her as long as possible. "Say you will marry me, and I'll share with you more of what you can come to expect from me as a husband."

Isadora rested her forehead against his chest. "Oh, how I want to…but I can't. I can't think straight, and Minerva always says…" She shook her head and peered up at him. "Never mind what Minerva would say. I promise to give you my answer tomorrow. Will that suffice for now?"

"Aye." He wasn't angry, nor was he disappointed. Oddly, he admired her for her strength to say no. "Let's get you home safe. We can discuss this after we've both had a good night's sleep." Only he knew he wouldn't be sleeping much, and probably wouldn't be until he made her his wife, and she occupied his bed every eve. He wanted to hit himself on the forehead for sounding exactly like his papa.

CHAPTER FOURTEEN

LAUGHTER PEELED DOWN to the foyer of Lord Torrance's residence as the clock chimed the hour. Ten o'clock. Tom was on time, but not early, which would aggravate his mentor to no end. He shrugged out of his greatcoat and handed it over to the butler who was smiling. His staff never revealed any type of emotion in his presence. He'd spied a smirk or two from the Avondale staff when Charlotte was about, and they weren't aware he was near.

Charlotte. She had been the mistress of Avondale for years, well before her time to run a household. With him often absent, she had assumed the role and managed the estate with a maturity well beyond her years. If he married, she would be relieved of the burden. She deserved a year or two of freedom, and he'd gladly bear the burden of funding multiple Seasons in order to make his sister happy.

The butler swung the door open, and Tom froze at the threshold at the sight of... mayhem. Torrance carried one small boy on his shoulders as he prepared a plate at the sideboard. Another dark-headed child of the same age sat upon Lady Ethel's lap and was stuffing a muffin in his mouth while his mama rocked a cradle next to the table.

"Ah! Your Grace, is it ten already? Do come in and stop loitering in the doorway." Lady Ethel nodded to a chair next to her.

"Have you broken your fast this morn?"

He shook his head. He rarely ate before the noon hour. "Not this morn."

"Nerves can kill an appetite," Torrance said as he offered Tom a plate. "Welcome. We prefer casual dining when the children accompany us to Town."

Tom accepted the plate and proceeded to scan the sideboard, hoping to find something that would dislodge the lump that had formed in his throat. He was rarely at a loss for words, but the scene before him evoked memories from his own childhood that he had buried long ago. He placed poached eggs, a corner of sliced bread, and a couple of pieces of ham on his plate before sliding into the seat Lady Ethel had motioned to.

"Well, Your Grace, it is with a heavy heart that I shall inform you that Captain Bane is expecting you to present yourself at four this afternoon. Don't be late."

The bitter taste of failure held him mute.

Torrance settled his son in the chair next to Tom. The young boy was a spitting image of his brother. Both boys shared Torrance's wavey chestnut hair and square jawline, which left no doubt as to who had fathered them.

"Ye a real duke?" the lad asked.

"Aye, I'm the Duke of Avondale." Tom nodded and made a mock bow in his seat.

Mouth half-full, the other mite slid from Lady Ethel's lap and tugged on his brother's arm. "Time to go."

"I don't want to go see the nanny. I want to watch papa question His Grace." Despite his objections, the boy followed his brother out of the room.

The door latch fell into place, and Torrance said, "Captain Bane predicts you should reach Calais before dawn if the winds are favorable." Tom's host slid his hand under his waistcoat and extracted an envelope. "If all goes well, you should return in time for the Fairmont ball and resume your pursuit for a duchess."

Both Torrance and Lady Ethel were acclaimed as excellent

judges of character. They weren't easily deceived. Why then did Tom feel affronted that they had not believed he had already fallen in love with Isadora? Confused. Would marrying Isadora be a love match or a marriage of convenience?

He withdrew the parchment with his orders from the envelope and scanned its contents. Switching his gaze between Torrance and Lady Ethel, Tom said, "How do you expect me to obtain such intel?"

Lady Ethel's brow creased. "By the usual means. You are the master of extracting intel from the spouses of our enemies, and Comtesse Du Montford has a particular fondness for tall, dark handsome gentleman."

"Then why not send your husband?"

Lady Ethel retorted, "Because he is married, and you are not."

"But I intend to be, and I..."

"The assignment should not interfere with your plans, that is if our intel is correct," Torrance offered.

"What intel?"

"We discovered that it is your intent to enter into a marriage of convenience with Lady Isadora Malbury."

"That was my original intent...until..." Tom cringed as a high-pitched wail came from the crib.

"See husband!" Lady Ethel stood to pick up the baby and cradled it in her arms. "I was correct, Avondale wasn't feigning the adoration I saw in his gaze when he danced with Lady Isadora. He may have set out believing a marriage of convenience is what he sought, but then he was struck by love."

"Wife."

"Husband."

Tom observed a battle of wills between the couple. Tom took another bite of his toast and nearly choked on the bread when he realized he was the reason for the discord between the couple. What was wrong with him, instigating a fight between the loving couple? How selfish of him. He rose from the table and neither of his hosts paid him any mind. "Torrance. Lady Ethel. I shall bid you both a good day. I have much to attend to before I set sail."

"Ha!" Torrance reached out and took the sleeping child from his wife. "I told you he would place duty before love."

Lady Ethel's jaw dropped for a moment and then she quickly snapped, "You just cost me a week's worth of nappy changes and two months' worth of pin money."

Aghast, Tom replied, "Torrance change a nappy? That's what the nanny is for."

"Regardless, those were the terms of our wager." Torrance smiled, opened the door, and marched out to the hall.

Tom bowed. "My apologies, Lady Ethel."

"You best figure out a way to obtain the information we need without using the art of seduction, or you will never know what it would be like to wake up next to Lady Isadora every morn. She will not marry a philanderer like her papa."

"I shall heed your advice, Lady Ethel, and when I return, I shall find a way to make it up to you."

He grabbed his coat from the butler's arms as he strode out to his waiting carriage. He was halfway home when he tapped on the roof and called out, "Malbury residence."

He needed to notify Isadora of his departure in person and gain her promise not to accept another's offer until he returned. Scandals could happen in a blink of an eye, and he'd be abroad for at least a full week if not two.

CHAPTER FIFTEEN

THE RATTLE OF carriage wheels out the front window of the Malbury residence had both Isadora and Minerva glancing at each other and then through the sheer curtains.

"Are you expecting a visitor?" Minerva asked.

Fantasizing about Tom wasn't the same as expecting him. Isadora shook her head, both in denial and to clear her thoughts of Tom's warm body. "No. You?"

Minerva narrowed her gaze. Her sister didn't believe her. She wouldn't have believed her since her cheeks were warm with guilt.

"The carriage is marked with the Avondale crest," Minerva said, still staring out the window.

The man she'd been secretly hoping to see all morning was about to walk through the door, and her mind went blank.

Isadora's breath caught as Mr. Morris announced, "His Grace, the Duke of Avondale, requests an audience with Lady Isadora. Are you in, m'lady?"

"Aye, please show His Grace in." She caught the butler's glance at Minerva, who nodded. All night, she considered Tom's arguments to say yes. To be the mistress of her own home. Her say would be final without needing the support of her elder sister. She'd never really considered such things before and, after thinking about it, it grated on Isadora's nerves that the staff still looked to Minerva for confirmation. It wasn't the staff's fault; they were doing their jobs.

Minerva remained by the window. "I shall remain to chaperone, however, pretend I'm not here."

"That shall be rather hard to do." Her response garnered her a scolding stare from her sister. Becoming mistress of her own home was becoming a rather strong argument in Tom's favor.

Mr. Morris announced, "His Grace, the Duke of Avondale."

Tom entered, and Isadora rose and dipped into a curtsey.

"Lady Minerva. Isadora." He bowed and then continued to stand within an arm's length of Isadora. "I suppose, Lady Minerva, there is little chance of having a private moment with your sister."

"Not here, and not this morn." Minerva turned to peer out the window as if the empty street was the most fascinating sight.

"Very well." Tom inched closer, teasing her with his warmth. Unthinking, she took a half step back. Tom's brow crinkled for a moment. For years, she had no desire to be close to another, except now she craved the warmth of Tom's presence.

Isadora shuffled forward, eliminating the space she had placed between them. Yet, he remained a tad too far away from her. She wanted to feel his hands upon her, to wrap her arms about his neck and bring his lips… She stopped her line of thought before she acted upon them.

Tom leaned in to whisper, "I must journey to France." His breath skimmed over the skin of her neck that he had tasted and nibbled upon hours ago.

From the corner of her eye, Isadora spied Minerva opening her mouth, but before she could say a word, Tom eased back a step and he continued loud enough for Minerva to hear without straining. "We shan't be able to complete the remaining two events before the commencement of the Season, thus I've come today to inform you I forfeit my claim to Wembly Hall."

The fog over her mind lifted. Tom's words sunk in—he was leaving. She knew better than to inquire as to why he was leaving in front of Minerva, for he'd not be able to disclose the real reason anyway.

Infusing delight into her voice, Isadora said, "The Wicked Ladies will be pleased to hear I've secured our location once again for the entire Season." She should be filled with joy. She'd accomplished the task, and her decision whether or not to seriously consider Tom's proposal was no longer a pressing matter. She had asked for time, and time is what she received.

Wasn't that what she wanted?

Isadora raked her eyes over the man before her. Tom was attractive both inside and out. He exuded masculinity she recognized that women would find hard to resist. She herself found herself immune to all others but the Duke of Avondale. Did Tom's missions require him to employ his charms to obtain intel or gain the enemy's trust? Isadora's breath caught in her chest at the thought. Now that she considered the matter, marrying a spy might not be the adventure she was looking for after all.

She wanted…she'd find a man who preferred the country, a recluse like her sister Diana had. No. A recluse wouldn't do. She enjoyed being in London far too much for that. Mayhap a man more like her brother Benedict. No. His scientific experiments had him holed up in his lab for days. She wanted… Hmm… Did she know what type of man she would be willing to sacrifice her freedom, her membership to the Wicked Ladies Salon for?

Her gaze collided with Tom's. Isadora forced the corners of her lips up to form a smile.

Tom returned the gesture and said, "Grand." Lowering his voice he continued, "I hope you are happy. I'll be receiving an earful from my peers when they discover we shall have to convene near the docks this year."

She didn't want to talk or think about the upcoming Season. She wanted to ask him why he was leaving for the Continent? When did he expect to return? Why was he leaving so suddenly? Her mind continued to formulate a multitude of questions.

When Tom raked his hand through his hair, she noticed the lines of worry at the corners of his eyes. The man was clearly distraught. He might be facing a life-or-death situation, and here she was standing beside him, wrestling with thoughts she already knew futile.

She wanted to see his smile, for it might be the last time she saw him. "Hmm… And here I thought the added element of danger would appeal to the gentlemen of your set." Her eyes widened as the double meaning hit her.

Tom grinned and chuckled. "Mayhap you are correct. If I phrase the news carefully, they might indeed be willing to traverse across Town to partake in…"

"In?" She wagged her brows at him.

"In vice and folly. Although I won't admit to having said that."

"Your secret is safe with me."

"And despite my better judgment, I believe you." He bowed and said full-voiced, "A good day to you, Lady Isadora." He spun on his heel and left.

Lady Isadora. The use of the honorific implied that he was distancing himself. Which was for the best. He was leaving, and she had much to do. Then why did her chest ache and her stomach feel as though she needed to retch?

Minerva wrapped her arms around Isadora. "He'll return, and hopefully by then, you will have sorted out in your mind what it is you want."

"I know what I want. Freedom to partake in activities that provide me joy. Marriage to any man, let alone to a duke, would only hinder me, not grant me more freedom."

"Is it really freedom that you seek? You have the luxury of partaking in numerous scandalous activities now, more than what most ladies would even dare to dream of, yet you still are searching for…well that is for you to determine. I suspect merely being in Avondale's vicinity sparks ideas. Although it appears that you are not ready to admit to the influence His Grace has upon you."

As stealthy as she had moved to embrace Isadora, Minerva released her and moved back to peer out the window at the empty street. "It's rather quiet in Town when the Season is not in full swing. I rather like it."

Drake's words from the prior evening echoed through her thoughts. *She's planning something...something extremely complex.* Over the years, Isadora and Diana had debated the likelihood of Minerva scheming to disappear.

Was it possible to hide in plain sight?

If anyone could achieve it, it would be Minerva.

With Tom gone, Isadora could refocus on the Wicked Ladies Salon and keep close tabs on her sister. Those were the things that mattered, not the dull ache in her chest that appeared as soon as Tom had left.

CHAPTER SIXTEEN

WHERE WAS CHARLOTTE?

Tom stomped through the foyer of Avondale House. The answer to his quandary as to how best to conduct the mission without him having to share a bed with the enemy had hit him while his coach raced through the deserted streets of London after leaving the Malbury residence.

Tom ducked his head into the drawing room. Empty.

He moved into the music room. Empty.

He didn't have all day to play hide and go seek with his sister. He strode up to the nearest footman and asked, "Where in the hell is Lady Charlotte?"

"Your Grace, I believe your sister is in her reading..."

He didn't wait for the footman to finish. Tom swiveled and began to march toward the smallest room in Avondale Manor when a flash of Torrance's happy staff halted his progress. Urgh. He turned back around, and the footman, hot on his heels, nearly barreled over Tom.

Righting himself, the footman said, "Beg pardon, Your Grace."

"No, it is I who am sorry. I shouldn't have barked at you a moment ago." With a nod, Tom changed directions once more and strode down the hall. He reflected upon the befuddled look on the man's face. Damn and double damn. He had become the overbearing employer. Damn Torrance and his happy life. But after witnessing it firsthand and remembering that the Avondale staff used to smile when his parents were alive made Tom realize he still had much to learn about being a duke.

Without knocking, Tom strode into his sister's reading room. Sunshine spilled in through the wall of windows, and he found Charlotte sprawled out on the floor surrounded by maps and books with French titles. He tiptoed around the scattered papers and stopped in front of her. Hands behind his back, Tom peered down at Charlotte, who had yet to acknowledge his arrival. "We are to depart within the hour."

Rolling over onto her back, the book still in hand, Charlotte peered up at him as she placed the volume over her chest. "Where are we going?"

"France, aboard the *Quarter Moon*." Tom was beginning to second guess his plan as he struggled to reconcile the vision of his little sister before him and the female spy that could knock a man out cold.

"Hmm. What about your wish that I remain on home soil while you are on a mission?" Charlotte turned back over and rose to her knees to gather her items from the floor.

His knees cracked as he bent down. "I've decided that if you are old enough to marry, you are old enough to accompany me abroad."

Charlotte stopped stacking her books and stared directly at him. "Tell me the real reason you are allowing me to accompany you."

Having never lied to his sister in the past, he wasn't going to start now. "I'm unwilling to employ my usual tactics to extract the intel from Comtesse Du Montford. I need your help."

"Ahh...so you need my help. Was it that difficult to say? I'll assist you if you answer my next question. Why are you unwilling to cuckold yet another member of the French aristocracy?"

Tom picked up the discarded books and placed them on the

table next to them. "Sister, language."

Charlotte tilted her head and arched an eyebrow. "Is it perhaps out of loyalty to Isadora?"

Flustered by the truth of his sister's words, Tom replied, "If you would rather not journey to the Continent with me, simply say so and I shall…"

"No need to concern yourself. I've been ready and waiting for you for near on two hours." Charlotte moved to the door and waited for him to join her. "I've already had our trunks sent down to the docks, they should be loaded by now."

He grinned at her audacity.

"I wanted you to confess to the real reason as to why you are willing to allow me to accompany you…on a ship, no less."

He hated crossing the channel. It always brought back childhood nightmares of his parents' last voyage. Tom motioned for her to exit and then followed close behind. "Is it so terrible I wish to spend as much time with you before your debut?"

She twirled around and poked him in the chest. "You've not cared an ounce about my pending debut." Charlotte turned her back to him and strode down the hall as she said, "You can lie to yourself, brother, but I wish you would refrain from attempting to deceive me. You are the only man I trust, and I'd hate for that to change."

She was right. She kept him honest. He lengthened his stride to catch up and when he did, he admitted, "You are correct. I'm seeking your assistance for some bloody illogical reason… out of a crazed need to be faithful to a woman who won't even deign to address me by my given name nor agree to a courtship. She's denied me multiple times, and yet I still can't stomach the idea of being intimate with another woman."

"Thank you for sharing your reasoning, brother. And since I adore Isadora and would love it if she were to become my sister, I'm happy to assist." Charlotte looped her arm through his and led him through Avondale House. "Let's discuss our strategy. I think we should…"

His sister continued to chatter while Tom came to terms with the truth. He was falling in love with a woman who he had to wager with in order to obtain her consent to escort her to four events. Over the years, he'd grown accustomed to women vying for his attention, and now it seemed the roles were reversed, and he didn't care for it. If Isadora refused him again upon his return, he'd simply have to find another woman to marry. His stomach knotted. It wouldn't be simple. And it wasn't a marriage of convenience that he truly wished for any longer.

Charlotte elbowed him in the ribs. "Do you think my plan would work?"

He hadn't listened to a word she had uttered or paid attention to the fact that they were already standing in front of his coach. Tom blinked and offered his hand to assist Charlotte up into the awaiting vehicle. "Let's review your plan once more on our way to meet Captain Bain."

Charlotte stared across the coach at him. "Since you were not listening to my plan, what are you thinking that has you scowling?"

He couldn't maintain eye contact with Charlotte. Eyes closed, he rested the back of his head against the coach wall. "I was thinking about Isadora."

After a minute or two of silence, his sister asked, "You're not worried she will become engaged while we are away, are you?"

Yes. Yes, he was, but there was naught he could do to prevent such a tragedy while hundreds of miles away. "If we complete our mission quickly, within a week or two, I believe..."

Charlotte kicked his ankle.

"Ouch."

"You want me to become Comtesse Du Montford's confidant within a week!"

Tom blinked at his sister in confusion. He really should have paid more attention to her plans.

Charlotte shook her head. "I'm affable, brother, but the comtesse will not simply share with anyone who her husband's consorts are. Plus, Isadora won't trade her membership to the Wicked Ladies Salon for anything less than love."

She was right on both points. Tom's shoulders relaxed. "I have faith in you, sister."

Charlotte leaned forward. "Do you believe there is any validity to the chatter regarding yet another escape by Napoleon? Escaping Elba was a feat, but to escape and return to Paris all the way from Saint Helena…is well, it's unfathomable."

"I won't know until we dock in Calais and I can investigate. This will not be an easy assignment, Charlotte. I need you to be on guard at all times and focused. We shall have to postpone further discussion regarding Isadora or the Wicked Ladies Salon until our return. Agreed?" He held his breath as he waited for his sister's reply.

"Agreed."

The coach rattled over wood slats. They were nearing the docks. He turned his focus away from the lady he was leaving behind and said, "Once we are aboard the *Quarter Moon*, let's discuss the details of the assignment and agree upon a strategy."

Charlotte nodded and turned to peer out the window, her hands tightly clutched in her lap.

Tom focused on the commotion outside. Men scurried back and forth, preparing ships for departure. Flags fluttered at the tops of masts. The tension in his shoulders returned. "Captain Bain is the best seaman in England, he shall see to it we make it to France and back safely."

"I don't doubt Captain Bane's ability." Charlotte pressed her palms to her stomach. "I hate sea travel."

Tom empathized. The combination of rolling seas and the memories of their parents' death made crossing the channel a terrifying experience. He let out a slow breath. "I'm glad you agreed to accompany me."

Charlotte continued to look out the window. "I'm happy you asked."

He had always worked missions alone, and now he was about

to embark on one of the most difficult assignments he'd been given with the aid of his little sister. Rather than dread, he was filled with optimism. They would be back before Isadora could miss him.

CHAPTER SEVENTEEN

ISADORA STOOD IN front of Mr. Wembly's desk and waited patiently as the landlord dipped his quill in the inkpot and dabbed the nib on a scrap parchment. She bit down on her tongue to refrain from yelling at the man to get on with it. Finally, he signed the blasted contract and blew on the parchment. Once the ink was dry it would be official. The Wicked Ladies would have exclusive rights to Wembly Hall for the duration of parliament, which was scheduled for the next five and a half months. Isadora should be elated at her triumph, but it was bittersweet, for she hadn't won it fair and square.

For nearly a week she had been tied up in negotiations with Mr. Wembly unable to enact upon any of the tasks required to prepare for the official opening night of the Wicked Ladies Salon. She filled her days with planning and devising lists all in an effort to banish Tom from her thoughts and her dreams. While she had succeeded in exhausting herself, she had failed at eliminating Tom from her mind both during the day and the night. She was constantly wondering what Tom was doing while away on Crown affairs. She hadn't expected him to send any correspondence, and none had arrived. Frustrated at her lack of progress on Wembly Hall and angry at herself for expending precious time and energy thinking about the man when he probably hadn't given her a second thought.

Isadora leaned to the side to peer out Mr. Wembly's office. With the curtains drawn back, she spied Minerva standing center stage looking out at the empty space before her. Isadora blinked and squinted at her sister. A peculiar feeling of familiarity prickled the back of her neck. Bah. She needed more sleep. Her eyes were playing tricks on her. For a moment in the midafternoon sun, Isadora thought Minerva resembled Madame Rosa the most highly sought-after opera singer that usually only crossed the channel to perform on British soil once or, on the rare occasion, twice a Season.

Mr. Wembly cleared his throat. "Wembly Hall is officially yours for the Season."

"My thanks and a good day to you, Mr. Wembly." Isadora took the signed lease and slid the parchment into the hidden pocket of her cloak.

Grumbling beneath his breath, Mr. Wembly stood as she turned to leave. Without a backward glance, Isadora left the man's office and climbed the side stage stairs, and froze. Her sister's lips were slightly parted, and the tip of her tongue peeked out of the corner. Minerva was scheming.

Isadora strode across the stage and stood next to Minerva. "The contract is all signed. We can return home now."

"I'm so proud of you. Championing the Wicked Ladies Salon is no trivial feat." Minerva smiled and gave Isadora a hug.

"My thanks for your vote of confidence, sister. I was beginning to wonder if Mr. Wembly and I would ever come to an arrangement." She looked over her sister's shoulder and scanned the room.

What had Minerva seen that had her mind preoccupied the entire time Isadora dealt with Mr. Wembly? Nothing appeared to be amiss or strange or out of the ordinary.

Isadora pulled back and Minerva released her with a quick last-minute squeeze. Minerva had been acting peculiar all week. Not once had she offered to assist with the negotiations with Mr. Wembley. Not once had she attempted to involve herself while

Isadora had paced about Minerva's chambers, complaining about the growing list of things to be accomplished. Not once had her sister mentioned Tom's sudden departure. It was as if her sister was distancing herself on purpose. Although Minerva had provided guidance on each and every task Isadora *sought* assistance with.

Arms looped, they made their way to the front doors. Halfway, Minerva turned and said, "I believe Mr. Wembly was trying to hold out for a better offer. While we know Avondale has adjourned to the Continent, there has been talk of His Grace's hasty departure. In fact, the gossipmongers are already at work. His Grace's appearance at the races has spurred whispers that this is to be the Season that the Duke of Avondale will find himself a bride. Which has given validity to the current rumor that after a day in the company of Misses, His Grace has taken up with his mistress until the Season officially begins and he gets himself leg shackled."

Isadora tensed at the thought of Tom being with another woman. "Why do so many ladies like mama simply turn a blind eye to their husband's infidelity? Not all marriages are contracted out of convenience or for money." Her voice held a tinge of sadness that she thought she had under control.

"I don't have a reasonable answer to your query. It's simply how things are." Minerva gave Isadora's arm a light tug. "Now come along, if we hurry, we might have enough time to stop by Gunter's and indulge in an ice."

Shuffling her feet, Isadora asked, "Would you agree to a marriage of convenience?"

Minerva's features transformed from indifference to contemplation, to abhorrence, back to indifferent all within a blink of an eye. "Regardless of whether I would or not, marriage is not in the cards for me, dear sister."

Minerva swung the large wooden door open and proceeded to their awaiting carriage. Isadora followed, and once they were seated side-by-side on the forward-facing seat, Minerva asked,

"Would you agree to a marriage of convenience?"

Isadora didn't know how to respond. She had pondered upon the question every night as she tossed and turned in bed. With a deep sigh, Isadora said, "I'll admit for a day…mayhap two, His Grace had me seriously considering his insane proposition. However, I've decided I'm not interested in a union in name only since there are no guarantees. While I've discovered that there are marriages that start off as merely a union of circumstance, and then the couples learn to love each other forming a bond so tight you would never have guessed that their union hadn't been a love match from the start…"

Minerva finished her thought for her. "There are those marriages like our parent's union, whose started off blissfully and is now a life sentence of misery for them both."

Isadora nodded and turned her attention to the buildings passing by, blinking away the moisture that built up in her eyes.

It was Minerva's turn to sigh. Her sister bumped her. "I see you have given this much thought."

"Aye. I have indeed." Isadora mumbled and then continued, "I believe I want a union like Diana's. I want to marry a gentleman that understands and loves me for all my faults."

Minerva grinned. "Nay. You need a gentleman that can afford your extensive wardrobe to back your debts, if necessary, to give you the freedom to quench your thirst for adventure." Her sister pinned her with a knowing stare. "You and I both know Avondale is the man that can give you all that and more."

"No. He can't." The rebuttal rolled off her tongue before she really gave Minerva's statement due consideration.

Minerva rolled her eyes. "Yes, Avondale can. You wish you could ignore the truth, but you can't—His Grace is your counterpart as Chestwick is Diana's."

Isadora let the silence fill the coach as they continued to rattle down the road. When she couldn't hold Minerva's stare any longer, she blinked and asked, "Is Drake yours?"

Her sister didn't even bat an eyelid. It was unkind to think of her sister as the Ice Queen, but Lord Mansville had picked a moniker that only her sister could warrant. "We are not discussing my relationship with Drake. That is all in the past and is no longer relevant."

No longer relevant? Isadora's heart raced. The finality in her sister's tone could only mean one thing—Minerva was on the verge of executing her plan. Which, in turn, meant Minerva was convinced Isadora was on the verge of marrying someone.

"I shan't be agreeing to a courtship with His Grace upon his return, let alone marrying the man."

Minerva shrugged and said, "You know I will support whatever decision you make."

This. This uncharacteristic response is what had Isadora panicking. "I do, and I shall reiterate my position once more—I will not marry before you."

CHAPTER EIGHTEEN

AFTER A LONG and drawn-out sennight of pretending to enjoy the company of his enemy, Tom sat across from his sister in his chambers. He was at his wit's end with their progress. Comtesse Du Montfort was either entirely ignorant or she was masterfully evading Charlotte's clever queries. He suspected the original information intercepted and passed along by the Foreign Office was inaccurate. Charlotte disagreed and remained convinced that, if given more time, she'd manage to obtain both the location and names of the remaining Napoleon supporters. The decision to involve his sister rather than execute the mission alone weighed heavily upon Tom's shoulders. Unable to summon the interest in the events occurring about him, Tom acknowledged he would be no further along if he had ventured alone.

Charlotte sat at the large wooden desk in the center of his assigned bed chamber. Twirling a quill back and forth between her fingers, she said, "These French imperial nobles are a rather complex lot. I'm not entirely certain that they remain loyal to Napoleon."

"Aye. The emperor had high hopes the imperial nobles would be a stable source of support for the regime." Unable to remain idle, Tom stood and walked over to the fireplace.

"Hence his strategy to grant a great number of titles. To think France has over thirty dukes, three to four hundred counts, and over a thousand or so barons. It has me confounded." His sister had poured over the guestlist for days, drawing an intricate diagram of how each individual was acquainted with one another and their association with their host, the Comte Du Montfort—who most naturally avoided. Comte Du Montfort had a darkness that cloaked him at all times. To Charlotte's frustration, Tom had not left his sister's side unless she was sequestered away with the comtesse along with the other women in the drawing room.

"It might be time we devise an alternate plan." Tom began to pace back and forth along the six-foot span in front of the fireplace. As a duke, he was assigned a rather lavish room in Du Monteford's home, which provided him and Charlotte plenty of room to work. "Although I still question whether or not we are on a fool's errand."

"I caught the comtesse making eyes at you last night at dinner." Charlotte's shoulders rolled forward as she sighed. "Perhaps it would be more effective if it were you who was pursuing the information we seek."

"Possibly." Tom turned and faced his sister. "If you were Isadora, would it bother you if I were to seduce a woman to carry out a mission?"

Charlotte placed the quill upon the desk and turned to fully address him. "Define seduction."

To hell and tarnation, he shouldn't be having this discussion with his sister, an innocent. "Forget I asked."

"Your cheeks are red. Don't be embarrassed, brother, I simply wanted to clarify to what extent you were willing to go in order to carry out your duties. I personally stop at kisses."

"Kisses! Who the hell dared to…"

Charlotte rolled to her feet and put her hands on her lower back and twisted to her right, then her left. She'd been seated at the desk for far too many hours over the past week. "Oh, don't be shocked." She wagged her brows at him and said, "So it's safe to assume that the seduction you are referring to then is more than kissing…."

"Bloody hell, how did we get on to this topic?" Tom raked his hand through his hair and then placed his clenched hands behind him. "Forget my query, and tell me who's the scoundrel that dared to take liberties with you? Tell me his name…" Charlotte's eyes widened, and he walked to stand in front of his sister. "Or is it names?"

Charlotte's lips thinned and she crossed her arms over her chest. "Calm yourself, brother. There shall be no dueling or fighting."

"Charlotte… I want their names." He gave her the ducal stare.

His sister covered the lower half of her face as she half snorted, half laughed.

"What is so amusing?"

"You are, brother. I intend to take the name, or shall I say names, to my grave."

"Oh, to your grave, you say?"

"Aye." His sister slipped back into the chair and scanned the parchment she had filled with lines and names. "Just as I'll take the knowledge of your actions to my grave if it becomes necessary for you to employ your charm and lure Comtesse Du Montford into your bed in order for us to complete the assignment and finally return to London."

"Trust me, I want to return to England as much as you, however, if I…" He suppressed the urge to be sick, his stomach in painful knots, and cleared his throat, then continued. "If I seduce Comtesse Du Montford, then I'll forfeit any chance of Isadora accepting my hand in marriage."

Distractedly, Charlotte replied, "It would seem you have a very difficult decision to make." The clock chimed the hour, and Charlotte jumped up from her seat. "I'm late." She rushed to his chamber door and stopped. "You stay and figure out what your next move shall be, and I'll be with the comtesse in the tearoom."

He moved towards the door. There's no way he would leave her unescorted. Charlotte lifted a hand in the air to stop him,

"Trust me and stay here."

She ducked her head out and looked both ways before looking over her shoulder at him. "Whatever you decide, I support you." And then in a flash, his sister was gone.

Damn female. It was hard to remain angry or frustrated at Charlotte when she was the only person in the world that loved him for who he was.

Restless, Tom resumed pacing about his chambers. This time he broadened his circuit. There had to be another way to gain the information they sought. The countess was beautiful in her own right, but his body didn't stir with interest, even in the slightest. He yearned to be close to Isadora again. He twisted at the waist as the latch rattled. He adjusted his breeches and banished the image of Isadora just as Comtesse Du Montford snuck into his room and leaned back against his door.

"You, monsieur are…" the woman waved her hands in the air as she searched for words. "I sent for you, and you… *Vous m'éludez.*"

"Elude you? No. I simply wished not to draw the attention of your husband."

She walked over to stand before him and trailed a finger along his jaw. "I do not believe you."

He had to make a decision—befriend the woman or seduce her.

He turned his head away to break the contact. When he turned back, he expected to be confronted with a frown or a look of scorn, but Comtesse Du Montford was smiling. "Since we last met, you have given your heart to another—*oui?*"

Tom found himself frowning. "Beg pardon?"

Footsteps in the hall had the comtesse scanning the room and rushing to hide in the adjoining changing room.

Charlotte reentered the room, muttering. "Bah. Halfway there and then stopped by a maid. A maid!" His sister walked over and leaned up against the bedpost. "Do you know what the maid said? Of course, you don't know. Well, she informed me that the comtesse has been delayed, and I'm to wait in my chambers." Shaking her head, Charlotte flopped back onto his bed and covered her eyes with her forearm. "I'm a failure. I've failed you, Tom. I'm so sorry."

Comtesse Du Montford emerged from her hiding spot. "You did not fail. You are very… brave."

Charlotte shot up to her feet. "Comtesse Du Montford." His sister's gaze fell upon him. "I didn't know…"

The comtesse wrapped Charlotte in a hug. *"Ne t'inquiète pas ma chère amie"*

His sister pulled back and asked, "You consider me a dear friend?"

"Oui." Their host extracted a note from the sleeve of her dress and tucked it into Charlotte's décolleté. "The staff…they cannot be trusted. I could not risk giving this to you in front of them."

Tom stepped up and winged out both arms for the ladies. "Shall we adjourn to the gardens?"

Comtesse Du Montford shook her head. "Non. You go. Mademoiselle Charlotte and I will go have tea now."

Tom nodded and left his room, leaving the two women behind. He had much to think about. Specifically, the comtesse's statement about him having fallen in love. Was it really that apparent?

God, he hoped not. If he was that transparent, then his effectiveness as a spy was over.

CHAPTER NINETEEN

P ASTEL PINK, GREEN, and blue silk gowns, alongside stockings and garters, and an array of wraps littered Isadora's chambers—on her bed, over her reading chair, and draped across the top of her chest of drawers. It was a disaster.

Minerva stood behind Isadora, playing lady's maid. "Promise to be careful tonight."

"If you were accompanying me instead of Drake, there would be no need for me to promise, now would there." Isadora sucked in another breath as Minerva tugged on the dark mauve ribbon wrapped tight about her chest. She glared at Minerva over her shoulder. "Stop worrying, it's a private masquerade party, and I personally vetted each invitation."

"But with each attendee donning a domino, you cannot be certain. Promise me." Minerva had been on edge all evening.

"I promise." Isadora twirled around and wrapped Minerva in a hug. "You have naught to worry about. Drake won't leave my side."

Minerva pulled back. "With Benedict and Diana married, and Gregory and Paul away at school, who else am I going to worry about?"

Isadora imagined wringing Drake's neck for the thousandth time. Minerva should already be married and caring for her own babies, not playing the role of a spinster sister and worrying over her siblings.

Minerva spun around and shifted through a pile of shawls. "Who did Charlotte list as her guest?"

"Her brother." Isadora's heart faltered, skipping a beat at the thought of being in the same room as Tom. Riddled with anxiety and desire to see the man, Isadora was in a constant flux of emotions.

She avoided Minerva's gaze but noted her sister's half-hearted attempt to mask a smile. The corner of Minerva's lips twitched. "I'm surprised the Duke of Avondale didn't appear on our stoop the eve of his return."

Tom and Charlotte had returned to London three days ago. He had sent Isadora a note the first eve they were home, informing her he would come to see her as soon as possible. But instead of Tom appearing at the Garnett affair she attended, she received another missive from His Grace informing her he had been detained by the Head of the Foreign Office for questioning. She had collected two days' worth of brief but poignant notes all stating he was sorry for the delay. Excitement coursed through her and continued to build as she counted down the hours until the masquerade. She craved Tom's touch, and his touch only. She knew this to be true since she continued to instinctively shy away from all other gentlemen.

Minerva grabbed a shawl that matched the same dark coloring as Isadora's domino and moved to stand behind her once more. She secured the domino over Isadora's eyes and nose—the silk fabric was soft against Isadora's cheeks that were aflame from the mention of Tom. With the mask in place, a surge of confidence flowed through her. She could face Tom without fear. "His Grace, I'm sure, had more important matters to attend to than paying us a social call."

"Perhaps." Minerva twirled Isadora by the shoulders. "You need a husband who matches you in intellect, shares your perspective on life, and who will love you passionately and unconditionally."

"And you believe Tom could be that man?"

Her sister gave her a little push. "Aye, I do. Now, go enjoy your evening."

Isadora ambled toward the door. With her hand resting on the latch, Isadora asked, "Dare I ask what your plans are for the evening?"

"I shall be here."

Isadora wanted to roll her eyes at the lie, but she refrained and instead stared directly at Minerva and said, "I don't believe you. There is a reason why you wanted Drake preoccupied this eve. You didn't want him following you wherever it is you are going."

"Since when have you become so perceptive?" Minerva bustled about Isadora's bed chamber collecting all the rejected dresses.

"Merely because I choose to pretend not to notice your peculiar behavior doesn't mean I'm not aware." Isadora searched her sister's features. The stubborn set of Minerva's jaw meant her sister was not going to share her plans.

Finding out Minerva's secrets would take more time than she could afford this eve. Drake was waiting for her. Isadora opened her door and crept down the hall.

Escaping into the night through the terrace doors, Isadora welcomed the chill.

Drake stepped out of the shadows. "Did she share her plans?"

"Don't be daft. Whatever Minerva has planned, she wants no interference from us. However, I see no reason why you must remain at Wembly Hall for the duration of the ball."

She stared at her eldest brother's best friend. "For the past two and a half Seasons, I believed Minerva's challenge to only wed the man who could best her in a game of chess was simply a device to allow my sister to have a say in who she would marry. However, earlier she told me I should seek out a husband that matches me in wit and intelligence with such conviction that I've reconsidered. Her declaration might be simply a way for her to discover if there is an eligible gentleman who could match her intellect. Which means sadly, even if you did love her, she probably wouldn't marry you."

"Are you calling me a dunderhead?"

"I'd never do such a thing." Isadora stepped up into the carriage waiting in the alley. "It would take a genius to defeat Minerva in a game of chess, and you, my dear old friend, are no genius."

Ignoring her statement, Drake smiled and crossed his arms over his chest. "If Avondale wishes to resume his pursuit of you, will you agree to a courtship?"

Her attempt at igniting Drake's fury fell upon deaf ears. The man, who was like a brother to her, was his stubborn laissez-faire self. Drake was equally stubborn as her sister and never heeded the wisdom others tried to impart to him.

Isadora mirrored Drake's pose and crossed her arms over her chest and huffed. "What does it matter to you?"

"I care about you as if you were my own sister." Drake unraveled and leaned his elbows on his knees and clasped his hands together. Looking at his hands and not at her, he continued, "I want you to be happy and safe. I shall support you as best as I can."

"You sound like Minerva."

Drake glanced up at her. "I'll take that as a compliment since I know you hold your sister in high esteem."

Isadora had wanted to discuss her dilemma with Minerva, but her sister was in no position to give her an unbiased opinion. She stared at Drake's bent head. Her married siblings, Benedict and Diana, would not arrive for another week, and Drake was offering to listen and help her muddle through the evening. Sending up a quick prayer for patience, she said, "I fear what Minerva will do if I agree to allow Tom to court me."

"So, you really don't know what she is up to this eve?"

"Of course, I don't." This was futile. The man *was* a dunderhead. She pressed her back into the coach seat, closed her eyes, and let her mind race through all the advantages and disadvantages of spending time with Tom.

"Actions out of fear are never as fruitful as those that are driven by purpose." Drake's slow and thoughtful response filtered through Isadora's thoughts.

"I would agree, however, the uncertainty of how my actions shall impact Minerva outweighs any of the logical reasoning for or against Tom." Isadora rubbed her temples which were beginning to ache.

"If you place your concern for your sister's welfare aside, what would you do?"

"I'm still undecided."

Drake sat up and tilted his head until he captured her gaze. "I'm not asking what you think you should do, I'm asking what your instincts are telling you to do."

Isadora frowned at his statement. "I'm not one to act on impulse and you know that."

"Mayhap it is time you did." Drake arched a quizzical brow at her.

"That is ridiculous! I hardly know Tom. He barely spoke more than five words to me the entire time we attended his house party late in the summer. And...I've been in his company less than a handful of times since, and each occasion has evoked nothing but conflicting thoughts within me."

"Thoughts or reactions?" Drake asked.

Blast the man for knowing her so well.

He continued to ask, "Do you find Avondale pleasing to the eye?"

"What woman doesn't?"

"Valid point." Drake sat back and crossed his legs, resting his ankle on his knee. "Let's approach this from a different perspective." His foot bounced, a sign he was deep in thought. Drake was taking this discussion seriously. He was honestly trying to help her. Despite his lack of care for Minerva's heart, Drake was a good man. Her brother's best friend was a constant guest at

Malbury Manor despite him owning the estate next door. In fact, growing up, he was the one that encouraged her to evaluate risks and take chances.

Should she trust her intuition about the duke?

Drake's foot stilled. "Rather than agreeing to a courtship, which has a certain element of uncertainty, would you agree to marry Avondale?"

"Are you suggesting the reason why I'm hesitant to agree to courting is due to ambiguity?"

"I am."

Could Drake be right?

There was something about Drake tonight that was different. He appeared older, wiser, and… serious.

He deserved a thoughtful answer, not one of the more flippant retorts she was accustomed to giving him. "Now that I consider it, the risk of losing Minerva to whatever scheme she's planning for a mere courtship does not appeal."

"I would agree." Drake straightened and switched seats and sat next to her. "If Avondale proposed this eve, what would you say?"

"Drake, you know I hate repeating myself." She clenched her hands and said, "It would be folly to say yes to a man I barely know."

"What more do you need to know? You are already privy to one of Avondale's most heavily guarded secrets. He does not share that with merely anyone. He trusts you."

"It's not much of a secret if everyone knows about it."

Drake shook his head. "The only reason I know Avondale's secret is because the Head of the Foreign Office sent him to recruit me."

"Oh." Isadora frowned. Who was this man next to her? "You're a spy?"

"Most definitely not." Drake returned her stare. "You've known me all your life. Do you think I could be a spy?"

She narrowed her gaze and studied Drake for a moment.

"Now that I think upon it, yes. Yes, you could be."

"Well, I assure you I'm not." Drake glanced out the window. "But enough about me...we were talking about you and Avondale."

"Right." Isadora gathered her scattered thoughts. "Is trust enough to build a marriage upon?"

"It's a far better foundation than lust."

Drake was right. Her parents' marriage had begun with lust and then disintegrated to nothing because of a lack of trust.

She turned and awkwardly wrapped Drake in a hug. "Thank you for helping me decide."

Drake patted her back in a brotherly manner. "I'm coming to realize it's best to obtain verbal confirmation when it comes to women's thoughts. What exactly have you decided?"

Isadora laughed and pulled away. "You'll have to wait and find out. Avondale should be the first to know of my decision, wouldn't you agree?"

Drake tugged at his coat sleeves and shifted back into the rear-facing seat, giving her the personal space she preferred. He knew her well. "You shall make an excellent duchess, but even more importantly, an exceptional agent for the Foreign Office."

Drake's compliments were filled with sincerity. She would make an excellent agent for the Crown.

But would Tom agree to wait to be married? Isadora wanted to see Minerva wed first.

CHAPTER TWENTY

Back home safe, surrounded by staff that were smiling, Tom stood in the middle of the Avondale foyer. He was looking forward to this evening's masquerade ball. Why the bloody hell was Charlotte taking so long to get ready? He pulled out his father's pocket watch and glanced down at the timepiece. Only another hour and he'd once again be in the same room as the woman he wanted to call wife. Staying away from Isadora while he dealt with his duties at the Foreign Office had taken a toll on Tom's nerves. Coupled with the fact that Charlotte had been bouncing about the house with glee at her official invitation to join the Wicked Ladies Salon all day.

After a successful mission, he would have thought gaining entrance to the woman's network would pale in comparison. It wasn't wrought with danger and… his train of thought vanished as he beheld a mature young lady in a rich, forest-green velvet dress descend the stairs. A matching domino fell from his sister's wrist. Charlotte was no hoyden tonight. No, she was poised, elegant, and the spitting image of their mama.

Tom's hands instinctively clenched by his side. He'd have a hell of a time keeping the gentlemen away from her tonight. When she reached the last step, Tom said, "Sister, mine, you look…"

"Beautiful. Gorgeous. Like our mama?"

Tom blinked, the moisture threatening to appear in his eyes. "Aye. Just like mama." He held out his hand and said, "Shall I accompany you and Aunt Cornella tomorrow to court?"

Instead of taking his hand, she shook her head. "Nay. Aunt Cornella and I already met with the Queen. She privately bestowed her endorsement of my debut."

"When did this occur?"

"While you were sequestered away by the Head of the Foreign Office yesterday." Charlotte produced a folded parchment from behind her. "We also managed to obtain this." She handed him the parchment marked with the seal of the Archbishop of Canterbury.

A special license. He accepted her gift. "My thanks, sister. This must have cost you at least a month's worth of pin money."

"Two, in fact." Charlotte stepped down to come to stand next to him. "And…it took all of Aunt Cornella's connections merely to get a meeting with the archbishop and then she had to wield her charm as I've never seen her do before to have him even consider issuing the license. Apparently, marrying by special license is simply not done by dukes."

"I shall have to send around a note of thanks to dear old Aunt Cornella for her assistance."

"Oh, she's expecting both you and Isadora tomorrow to join her for luncheon." Charlotte stepped forward and pulled her hood over her perfectly arranged coiffure and began to make her way out the front door.

"What if Isadora abhors the prospect of sharing a life with a spy? What if…"

His sister didn't even pause at his questions. She simply continued on. He lengthened his stride to catch up to her and assist her up into the coach. "Did you hear my concern?"

"Oh, I've heard them plenty since we returned. But you won't know the answers to any of your worries unless you speak directly to Isadora. I've done my part, now you must do yours."

They were a team. If Charlotte had faith, then so should he.

"Perhaps I could recruit Lady Minerva's help this evening."

Charlotte shook her head and said, "I'm afraid not. Lady Minerva will not be attending this evening's festivities."

"Who's Isadora's guest then?"

"Lord Drake. Isadora made the mistake of wagering on a game of rummy with her sister." Seated in the coach, Charlotte pushed back her hood and loosened the string of her cape. "It was Minerva who suggested Aunt Cornella and I pay a visit to the archbishop. Does that knowledge help ease any of your concerns?"

"Nay. I don't want Isadora to feel as if she was coerced into marrying me." Tom settled back into his seat and rapped on the coach roof, setting it into motion. Was he ready to declare his love to Isadora?

"I'm fairly confident Minerva did not share her plans with Isadora." Charlotte tapped his knee. "Did you hear me?"

"Yes. Yes. Isadora is unaware of her sister's contingency plan." Tom ruminated for a moment and then added, "It's a wonder the Crown hasn't approached Minerva to join the Home Office."

Charlotte gave him a lopsided smile. "What makes you believe they haven't? It could simply be she has declined in the past due to family obligations."

Tom asked, "Such as?"

"Seeing to it that her two younger sisters were happily wed." Charlotte grinned and then continued to say, "You did ask that I investigate Minerva's background, did you not?"

"I did, but that was only three days ago." Since they had returned, he had spent most of his waking hours at the Foreign Office reviewing the wealth of intel that Comtesse Du Montford had provided. With Torrance's aide, they had developed a strategy, albeit a complex strategy, to infiltrate the thin but broad remaining Napoleon support network. After seeing the benefits of having a partner on the last mission, all of Tom's ideas had involved Isadora accompanying him back to France. He never wanted to venture that far from her ever again.

Charlotte broke his train of thought. "Aunt Cornella is surprisingly well connected. I think I shall reside with her for a spell after you recite your nuptials."

Tom didn't love the idea of Charlotte not residing under the same roof as he. "I suppose you've already made arrangements."

"I have."

He looked at his sister once more. She was all grown up. She was no longer in need of him. A pang of guilt at not having spent more time with her spread throughout his chest.

Charlotte patted his knee. "Don't look so sad. It's not like I'm getting married and never returning to reside with you and Isadora."

"That's still a possibility. You know Aunt Cornella loves to play matchmaker."

"Bah. It'll take much more than handsome features and sweet words to convince me to marry."

Interesting. "What exactly do you think women look for in a husband?"

"You have to figure that out for yourself, dear brother. However, in your case, might I suggest you employ your skill at cards to impress Isadora?"

"Are you suggesting I gamble on my future?"

"Aren't you the one that always says it's skill, not luck, that determines the outcome of certain card games?"

His sister's plan had merit. But for the first time, he was going to approach the evening without a plan and simply take his lead from Isadora. His trip with his sister proved he did not have to be in control for things to work out.

CHAPTER TWENTY-ONE

THE ORCHESTRA COULD hardly be heard over the roar of excited chatter. The Wicked Ladies were in fine form tonight, all eager to gather after being ensconced at their summer residences. Isadora stood at the entrance of Wembly Hall, greeting members as they arrived.

Drake touched her elbow and whispered, "It is time for our dance."

"But I should remain here and…"

He didn't let her finish her sentence. "Let's celebrate your success and stop milling about the entrance waiting for His Grace and his tardy sister to arrive." He urged her forward with a gentle push at the small of her back.

She frowned at Drake, not liking this authoritative version of her childhood neighbor. The obstinate set of his jaw had Isadora sighing and picking up her skirts. "Very well, if you insist."

"I do and, to be frank, I'm rethinking my earlier advice regarding Avondale." Drake's unusual curt tone spurred Isadora to wonder how well she really knew the man. Had Minerva ever witnessed this no-nonsense side of Drake?

Setting aside thoughts of Minerva and Drake for a moment, Isadora smiled and nodded at the Wicked Ladies Salon members and their guests as she made her way toward the dance floor. She noted that the space was barely occupied. Drake was right; she needed to set an example as Katherine had last year, needed to encourage engagement and participation.

Isadora turned and hoped Drake didn't detect the disappointment that suddenly hit her. She had hoped her first dance of the Season would be with Tom. Drake stepped closer but not too close and held an arm out for her. Despite being a close family friend, Drake wasn't one of her brothers, and her instinct to retreat was overwhelming. As if sensing her discomfort, Drake said, "Pretend that I'm Avondale. And I promise to keep my touch light."

She stepped up to place her hand on Drake's forearm as other couples moved to join them.

"Deep breaths. You'll do fine."

Drake's encouraging words, while well-meaning, had the opposite effect. Her entire body tensed. When Drake's muscle beneath her palm flexed, she flickered her gaze to him.

Scowling, Drake said, "If Avondale fails to arrive, I shall personally go in search of him and box his ears."

The brotherly sentiment had Isadora smiling and relaxing just as the music began. On cue, Drake led her through the country reel.

"Charlotte would not miss this event unless she had to attend to a pressing matter beyond her control."

"Agreed. But as for Avondale, he has no excuse."

As she fell into step beside Drake to promenade, she whispered, "When exactly did you become privy to Avondale's secret?"

"I've known for years." Drake shrugged. "His Grace makes it a point every year to summon me to Avondale for a chat."

"I don't understand. Why didn't you say yes?"

"Hard to believe, but I'm not the adventurous type." Drake bowed, then took her hand in his and placed his other hand upon her waist. He twirled them about the other couples.

As they weaved their way to the end of the line, Isadora said, "Liar. Tell me the truth, please."

"I have my reasons and let's leave it at that, so I won't attempt to lie to you." Drake scanned the room, as he had been throughout the duration of their dance.

Isadora stiffened and whispered, "They have arrived."

"Impressive that you can you sense his presence faced away and from across the room, no less."

"Don't be ridiculous. People don't sense each other's presence," Isadora lied. Her skin prickled along the back of her neck moments before Drake's reaction to seeing Tom alerted her to his arrival. Smiling at Drake's frown, she continued, "Your fingers tightened both at my waist and upon my hand as you glanced over my shoulder."

"Damnation. I thought I'd mastered hiding my reactions better than that."

"Why bother mastering the skill if you have no intention of accepting Avondale's proposition?"

"You, my dear, ask too many questions." He twirled her, switching their positions.

She glanced up to scan the room for Tom. He was slightly taller than most, so it should have been easy to spot him, but then Drake spun her once more. That was when she spied Avondale glaring at her.

⇒⇒⇒⟨⟨⟨⟨

THE ENTIRE INTERIOR of Wembly Hall had been transformed from drab to chic. The alterations hit a cord within Tom. She had brought about changes within him, too, all within a very short period. He searched the crowd for Isadora.

"Five o'clock," Charlotte said with a smile.

He shifted his gaze in the direction of the dance floor as his sister had suggested. Every rehearsed greeting fled Tom's mind as he stood, hands clenched at his sides. Isadora was in another man's arms, and the fact that the man was Drake only made his blood boil hotter.

Charlotte snapped her fan open and lifted it to cover the lower half of her face. With her domino covering the upper half no one would recognize her. She turned slightly toward him. Who was she hiding from? He peered over her shoulder and scanned the guests milling about. He didn't recognize half the gentlemen who donned dominos below. The possibility that Charlotte's behavior wasn't out of caution but due to fear hit him. "Are you nervous?"

"It's not the first time I've had to head into a sea of unknown individuals."

"True. But this time, it's not purely out of duty. You are personally invested. You want the women below to like you."

Charlotte's perfect posture faltered for a moment before she righted herself and said, "Now I understand why we are trained to remain detached."

"Our lives are extremely complex…and, at times, challenge us beyond what we believe ourselves capable. The past few weeks have proved that we are stronger, better agents when we work together. I'm here. For you."

"My thanks, brother, but tonight our mission is to get you engaged." Charlotte lowered her fan and snapped it closed. Once again, he was faced by his unstoppable sister. "You realize Isadora will not become any less attractive once you wed." Her gaze pointedly dropped to his hand that was still fisted at his side. "You had best become accustomed to the sight, and the idea that gentlemen will try to steal her away from you even after she has taken your name."

Charlotte was right. If he didn't want to find himself dueling every week and still remain effective on missions, he'd need to come to terms with the fact Isadora would no doubt draw the notice of both friends and foes.

He couldn't resist the pull to be closer to Isadora. Tom presented his arm to his sister and together they descended the stairs. "How do you think papa dealt with the fact mama drew such attention?"

"I'm sure it wasn't easy. However, it is irrelevant how he managed. It is the fact that he did, and their marriage did not suffer." Charlotte gave him a wink. "I have confidence you shall succeed, too."

He wanted to believe his sister.

The reality was he knew very little about Isadora. He was acting primarily upon intuition, driven by the fact that he no longer felt whole unless she was near. It was as if she reached into his chest and ripped out half of his heart and held onto it. With each step he got closer to Isadora, the stronger his heartbeat.

The music stopped, and Drake skillfully steered Isadora around so that they were facing each other. Drake's laissez-faire demeanor fell away as they approached. "A good eve to you, Your Grace. Lady Charlotte."

His sister dipped a quick curtsy, and Tom nodded. "Drake. Lady Isadora." His gaze remained on her.

She was breathtakingly beautiful. Her green eyes twinkled in the candlelight, and her deep burgundy silk gown had him yearning to taste her lips once more. Isadora removed her hand from Drake's arm, and the pressure in Tom's chest eased. Oh, how he longed to wrap her up in his arms and whisk her onto the dance floor. Drake bowed. The movement extracted Tom from his thoughts and reminded him he was in the middle of a crowded ball.

Hand extended, Drake asked, "Lady Charlotte, will you do me the honor of granting me this next dance?"

Charlotte took Drake's arm. "It would be my pleasure. We have much to discuss."

Isadora frowned at the pair as they weaved their way to the center of the dance floor. Fear that she was displeased at having been left with him alone had his airway tightening. Tom cleared the lump that had lodged in his throat. "Lady Isadora, would you care to dance?"

"Not particularly. I'm rather parched." Isadora's gaze tracked

Drake and Charlotte. "What is your sister up to?" She shifted closer to him and offered him her hand.

He placed her hand upon his arm and escorted her toward the refreshments table. When no one was close by, Tom leaned in and replied, "Charlotte intends to convince Drake to privately challenge Minerva to a game of chess."

She twisted, placing her lips inches from his. Was she testing his willpower? "What would Minerva stand to gain if she were to defeat Drake?"

It required every bit of his self-control not to whisk her into a nearby alcove and give into temptation. "His promise to not interfere with Minerva's plans to reinvent herself."

"Beg pardon." Isadora stopped short. "Reinvent herself? What do you know of Minerva's plans?"

Tom glanced to his left and then to his right. Thankfully, all the Wicked Ladies and their guests appeared to be preoccupied. "Charlotte suspects Minerva is planning on venturing to the Americas to assume a new identity. Your sister's name is on the manifest for the *Quarter Moon* that is scheduled to make the long journey in a month."

Brow furrowed, Isadora asked, "How did Charlotte discover such information?"

Tom boasted, "My sister is rather resourceful. She and Captain Bain have become close friends recently."

"Do you think Charlotte will succeed in convincing Drake to do what others have tried and failed?"

He straightened and smiled at the couple who passed by with quizzical looks. Tom urged Isadora forward, continuing toward the table lined with glasses filled with lemonade. "Aye. If he does not agree to issue the private challenge, Charlotte has been given permission to threaten him."

"Threaten him?"

"If he refuses to comply, Drake shall find himself aboard a ship bound for the West Indies at first light."

Isadora's hand tightened about his arm. "The West Indies?"

He glanced down to see her concern. Had Drake become more than a brotherly figure to Isadora while Tom had been away? "Aye, you heard correct."

Isadora nodded as they came to stand before the refreshment table. He procured two glasses and handed her one. Isadora appeared lost in thought as she lifted her glass to her lips and sipped. When she peered up at him, all signs of worry had disappeared, replaced with a glint Tom interpreted to be curiosity.

Isadora's lips curved and she asked, "What do you think of the renovations to Wembly Hall?"

It took a moment for her question to register. The sudden change in topics had caught him off guard, which was rare, given he was accustomed to conversing with Charlotte, the queen of redirection. He scanned the room and then her meaning hit him. With a wink, he replied, "Marvelous, but perhaps a tour of the establishment would enrich my appreciation."

Isadora curled her hand over his bicep, which instinctively flexed. "What a grand idea." She led him around through a curtain and down a candlelit corridor. They passed two doors before he felt his restraint snap. He halted in the middle of the hallway. "Where do the doors lead to?"

"A card room, a billiards room, a reading room, and the far door leads to my office." Isadora turned to face him. "Is there anyone, in particular, you would like to see first?"

The choice was obvious. "The card room."

"Very well." Isadora reached for his hand. It was the second time she had initiated contact, and the action had his heart swelling in his chest. He squeezed her hand, and she led him into the door to the right.

He opened the door to reveal six oval-shaped tables, all arranged with seating for six at each.

"Would you care to play?" Isadora tugged him toward a table that was lined with green felt like those found at gaming establishments. By Jove, she had created the female equivalent to

Brooks's, his gentleman's club. Grinning he answered, "I'm always up for a game of cards. What are the stakes?"

"If you win, I shall agree to a courtship. If I win, you shall grant me the answers to five questions I have regarding your involvement with the Foreign Office."

He would have happily agreed, but she would expect him to counter, and so he did. "Marriage…and three questions."

Isadora narrowed her gaze at him. "Shall we play Vingt en un."

Tom's heart nearly stopped at her eager acceptance. "Would you care to deal or should I?"

Isadora took her seat and reached for the deck of cards in the center of the table. "I'll deal."

Smart girl. He took the seat opposite her and sent up a prayer to Lady Luck, for Isadora handled the deck like a card sharp.

CHAPTER TWENTY-TWO

FANNING THE CARDS out onto the table in a straight line, Isadora flipped them over like dominos for Tom to view. It wasn't to prove she wasn't a card sharp; it was a show of trust. If trust was to be the foundation of their marriage, she wanted it to be solid.

Tom scanned the gaming cards and nodded for her to proceed. Scooping up the cards, she shuffled them, intermingling the rectangular pieces with a skill that she rarely displayed except in the company of family.

Her opponent eyed her moves carefully as if he were trying to read or memorize the order of the cards. She tilted the cards slightly downward, and Tom's brow creased. She piled the cards into a stack and pushed them toward Tom.

He removed his gloves, placing them on the seat next to him before he smoothly lifted the top half of the deck and placed it to his right. Isadora admired his sun-bronzed hands. Did Tom ride bare-chested and without gloves like her brothers during the warmer months?

Her cheeks warmed as her gaze settled upon Tom's chest. If she lost, she would find out soon enough. The thought had her blinking away her wayward thoughts, and she combined the stack to her right with the other. She asked, "How many rounds?"

"Until there are insufficient cards." Tom arrogantly cocked a brow.

An entire deck?

To track which cards had been played and how many court cards remained would require her absolute attention. She could not afford any distractions. Not one to rely on luck, she banished the images of a sun-kissed, bare-chested Tom seated upon a horse.

Focused, she dealt two cards, both face down. One in front of Tom and the other one in front of her. Inhaling deeply and concentrating on the cards before her, she dealt two more cards, this time face up. An eight of spades for Tom and a four of diamonds for her. Now came the tricky part, calculating the odds depending on Tom's next move.

He expertly lifted the corner of his bottom card and then waved his hand indicating he didn't wish for another.

Blast. She searched his face for a clue as to what card he held. His molten brown eyes gave her no clue but did manage to set her heart aflutter. His lips remained neutral, while the memory of his kisses had her shifting in her seat. She mustn't let her thoughts run amok. She stared at him for a moment longer. He must have a face card.

With her free hand, she peeked at her bottom card, and her heart skipped a beat at the sight of the seven of spades. She needed a seven or better to win. She flipped the third card over in front of her. A king of clubs lay next to her four of diamonds.

Tom groaned and asked, "What suit is your seven?"

She must have given away her card when she looked. She'd have to do better next round. Isadora smiled as she flipped over her bottom card. "Spades." She noted he stroked the table leaving a small mark in the felt. "Do you track suit or color?"

Tom chuckled. "I've attempted suit in the past, but playing a full deck, I can only manage color." He wiggled his fingers. Fingers she had fantasized about many times over the past fortnight. "I don't have enough digits."

Isadora shook her head. Concentration is what was required.

She needed answers before she committed the rest of her life to this man. "The odds of a tie are higher playing all fifty-two cards. May I suggest we simply play best of five."

"Now that you have won the first round, the odds are significantly in your favor to win if we play only five rounds."

She arched a brow at him. "Worried Lady Luck will not be on your side this eve?"

"Very well, best of five it is." He gathered the cards before them and placed them to the side.

Isadora dealt the next round. Both of them had face cards sitting in front of them. Tom was first to act; he motioned for another card, and Isadora flipped over a ten of hearts.

"I win." Isadora leaned forward and slowly turned over his concealed card. Could she divert his attention, as he had so easily distracted her?

She glanced down at the two of clubs. Shifting back in her seat, she revealed her bottom card—a nine of spades.

Tom wedged a finger into the folds of his cravat and tugged at the material until it came loose. His gaze lifted from her bosom to her eyes. "It appears Lady Luck is favoring you this eve."

"It would be grand if I were able to sweep the table, but the odds are actually not in my favor."

Ready to be done with the game, Isadora dealt both sets of cards face down this time. The added complexity would prove who had Lady Luck on their side. Tom again waved off the request for another card.

Isadora slowly lifted her cards. Five of hearts. Two of diamonds. She was a long way from twenty-one. Tom drummed his fingertips on the tabletop and a pang of desire rolled through her.

"I shall take a card." She dealt herself another card. Four of spades, making her total eleven. Mayhap Lady Luck really was on her side this eve. Her tongue peeked out the corner of her mouth and Tom shifted in his seat. "And one more."

Tom's brow rose, and she flipped over a three of hearts. Blast. She only had fourteen and the odds of a face card appearing next were extremely high.

Tom sat back and smirked. Damn the man, even his smirk had her pulse racing. She sighed, "And another."

As she expected, a face card appeared. Tom had won the third round.

He flipped over to reveal a six of diamonds and the knave of clubs. Isadora stared at the two cards. He only had sixteen. Had he asked for a card, he would have taken the four of spades and he would have had twenty and she… she would have had twenty also which would have resulted in a draw rather than a loss.

Tom leaned forward. "Is a loss that much worse than a draw in a best of five?"

With his cravat dangling loose, the top of his chest was exposed, confirming her suspicion the man rode bare-chested during the summer months.

Swallowing hard, Isadora replied, "Aye, it is."

Summoning all her willpower, she dealt the next round. She needed answers before she agreed to marry this man that set her blood ablaze. This time, she decided to deal the cards in the traditional manner, one face down and one face up.

She tried to ignore Tom's piercing gaze and focus on her cards. Tom brushed his thumb along the side of his card before he peeked at it. The memory of him trailing his fingers along her inner thigh had her clamping her legs together, but there was nothing she could do to stop the moisture pooling at her core.

Tom tapped his forefinger on the top of his cards, indicating his wish for another card. With the ace of hearts showing, he must not have a face card.

Heart racing, she flipped over another ace, this time the ace of clubs. Blast the man and his moniker—tonight he was the Duke of Aces. He waved off more cards, and Isadora turned her attention to her cards—king of hearts showing and hidden from Tom's view, a nine of diamonds.

Setting the cards down, Isadora declared, "I believe I'm good."

Tom flipped over the six of clubs.

She had won! She jumped to her feet. Elation at beating the Duke of Aces.

Tom rose and walked over to the settee in front of the fire. "I'm ready for your inquisition, my dear."

CHAPTER TWENTY-THREE

Hᴉs ꜰᴜᴛᴜʀᴇ ᴡɪꜰᴇ tread lightly. Tom had to concentrate to even detect Isadora's approach. She would make a fine spy—but would she want to be an agent for the Crown? His original plan for a marriage of convenience allowed for them both to lead separate lives, but now the idea of not sharing every aspect of his life left him feeling ill.

Standing before him with the glow of the fire behind her, Tom's mind cleared of all thought, and his pulse raced in reaction to the beautiful woman in front of him. He ached to reach out and disrobe her. Have his way with her. She was an innocent. An innocent with a very serious look set upon her features.

Isadora began to pace, tapping her forefinger to her lower lip. "Shall I begin?"

"Please do." Tom straightened his legs out in front of him and crossed them at the ankles.

"As a child, were you aware of your parents' activities?" She stopped a few feet away from him.

Interesting she would inquire about his childhood. With Isadora out of arm's reach, Tom was able to focus on his answer. "At the age of ten, my parents sat me down and had a rather frank discussion about the choices they had made and intended to continue to make. They gave me a choice: go to Eaton and make friends or remain at home and be tutored in preparation to join the Foreign Office. As a boy in his youth, I jumped at the opportunity to learn sleuthing and combat skills. It also meant I had to master how to dance, embroider, and become proficient at painting in watercolors."

"Embroidery. Watercolors." Isadora repeated. Her even tone revealed nothing of her opinions on either activity.

He rolled to his feet and took a step toward her. He needed to be closer to observe her reaction to his next statement. "Aye. Codes are embedded in pieces all the time."

His gaze fell to her décolleté as she wound her arms behind her back. "Hmm. What if your chosen bride is a miserable seamstress and terrible painter?"

"I shall tutor her myself." He forced himself to remain right where he was. He refrained from reaching out and grabbing her to him by the waist. Now was not the time to indulge in his wicked, wicked fantasies that plagued him each night.

Isadora rolled onto her toes and asked, "Do you always excel at everything?"

Damn, her sweet mouth was so close. She wished for answers, not kisses. Tom banished his devilish desires and answered, "I failed spectacularly at convincing you to allow me to court you." He meant it to be a teasing statement, but his words came out humorless.

With a slight tilt of her head, Isadora replied, "Is that so?"

The exposed skin of Isadora's neck had Tom clasping his hands tightly behind his back and inhaling deeply. Another mistake. The scent of lilacs set him on edge.

Isadora continued, oblivious to the effect she was having on him. "And here I thought you had decided not to pursue my hand after our private interlude." Isadora closed the gap between them and trailed a finger along the seam of his jacket.

She must think him a lout. "My apologizes, I should not have taken such liberties…"

Isadora placed a finger over his lips. "You have a tell, Your Grace, when you are lying, and I can see you are not one bit remorseful for your actions."

He wasn't. He waited for her to remove her finger and then wrapped his arms about her waist. Wishing he could reenact the night in his study, he let one hand slide lower to cover her lush bottom. "You are extremely observant. Share with me, what is my tell?"

She wound one arm around his neck. "Just before you utter a lie you clench your jaw and if I look closely here…" She brought her free hand up and placed a finger up to his temple and then ran it along his jawline. "I can see your muscles move ever so slightly."

"That's not why I was clenching my jaw." He spied a devilish twinkle in Isadora's gaze as she peered up at him.

"Why were you?"

He tugged her closer. "Standing inches from your lips takes every ounce of my self-restraint not to kiss you…I have to exert every shred of willpower not to drag you to the floor and have my way with you." The minx massaged the back of his neck.

"Ahh… I understand. Your gentlemanly honor prevents you from taking my maidenhead, but do you want to kiss me?"

"Yes." He dipped his head lower but not all the way. "I desperately want to kiss you, but first we need to address your concerns, and I need your agreement to marry."

Slinging her other arm around his neck, she stared into his eyes and said, "Very well, I shall ask my second question. Do you intend to continue to carry out your activities for the Crown after we are wed?"

Fear rippled down his spine. What was the right answer? He swallowed and spoke the truth. "I do."

She didn't step away at his answer, in fact, she brought his head down closer. "And my final question, if such activities take you abroad, will I or will I not be accompanying you?"

None of her queries were the ones he'd anticipated she might ask. He didn't have to think too hard on his answer. He wanted her with him, always. "It would be my preference for you to accompany me. However, if you would prefer not to, I would not force you."

She pressed her lips to his, and before he could dip his tongue to taste her sweet mouth, she pulled back and said, "I think I'm in love with you, Thomas Grandstone, Duke of Avondale, Earl of Harvey, and Count of Tourmaine."

"That is indeed good to know, for I am in love with you Lady Isadora Malbury." He brushed his lips over hers for a brief kiss. "Does this mean you will marry me?"

Isadora pulled back, "Aye, if it means you will kiss me, I agree to marriage." She stepped out of his hold and took his hand. Tom was certain they were headed back to the ball, but when she changed directions and led him over to the settee, he released a sigh of relief.

"Tom, please take a seat." It was the first time she had referred to him by his given name, and he didn't hesitate to do as she bid.

She didn't let go of his hand as he lowered himself onto the settee. Isadora stepped between his legs and dropped to her knees.

"Isadora, luv, what the devil are you doing?"

"Last time, you pleasured me until I reached my release. This time I want to pleasure you until you find your release."

His cock instantly hardened at her words and pressed uncomfortably against his breeches. She reached for the buttons on his falls. "Don't look so concerned. Chestwick Hall has a very extensive library. I studied the illustrations and believe it a fairly simple act. Although I'll admit, it was difficult to decipher if the males' faces were contorted as a result of pain or pleasure or a bit of both."

He rolled his eyes heavenward. Lady Luck was indeed on his side. How he came to be so fortunate as to find the perfect woman for him, he would never know. "Would you care for a little instruction from me, or would you prefer to have full reign?" He lifted his hips as she shimmed the waistband lower until his cock popped out.

She licked her lips and studied his engorged manhood. "A little instruction, please."

"Spit on the tip and then take me into your mouth as far as possible."

Without debate, she followed his instruction. He was in heaven. Isadora applied just the right amount of pressure with her lips as her mouth glided down his shaft.

"Good, pet, now bob up and down." His fingers weaved through her hair and tangled with the string of her domino. It wasn't long before he felt his balls tighten. He was close to release, but he was undecided if he should come in her mouth or into a handkerchief. He reached into his pocket for the handkerchief, and the motion drove him deeper. Isadora reached between his legs and stroked his balls and then squeezed. He tried to pull out, but her lips gripped him.

"Pet, your about to make me come, luv. I need to…"

She stroked him at the base of his cock, and it sent him over the edge. His cock jerked as he found his release. She swallowed and sat back with a wicked grin on her face. "Minerva always said it was just as pleasurable to give as it is to receive. I don't think I fully comprehended her meaning until now…now I understand."

God how he loved this smart, beautiful woman. He helped her up from her knees, and he pulled up his breeches so he wouldn't stain her gown when he tugged her to sit upon his lap. He bent and sought out her mouth for a kiss. "I want you. Promise to marry me as soon as possible."

"I promise to marry you, but not before Minerva is happily wed."

Tom pressed his forehead to hers. "What if it isn't marriage Minerva wants?"

"I know my sister. It is her greatest wish to become a mother. She must wed. If we work together, pool our resources, we could have her standing before a reverend in short order."

The idea of working together appealed to Tom. Then a

thought struck him, and he said, "If Charlotte succeeds tonight, and Drake wins the chess match, it won't be necessary for us to intervene." Tom would rather not play the role of matchmaker if at all possible.

"Even if Charlotte convinces Drake to issue the challenge, he won't win against Minerva. She may have loved him once, but her pride wouldn't let her throw a game, and Drake, well he hasn't played chess since we were children. There is no chance he'd defeat Minerva."

Tom didn't agree. Drake was a genius and, while it wasn't a foregone conclusion the insolent pup would defeat Minerva, Tom firmly believed it was a possibility.

Isadora curled and snuggled against him. "We should return to the ball."

"Aye." He agreed but neither of them moved.

He was content to simply enjoy having her close and in his arms. But they couldn't hide away the entire eve.

CHAPTER TWENTY-FOUR

TRAPPED IN THE spacious ducal coach as it rattled down the still dark cobbled streets toward her parents' townhouse, Isadora clasped her hands in her lap. She avoided Tom's gaze even though she could feel it upon her.

Drake had been pacing up and down the corridor in front of the billiards room when she and Tom exited the card room. Thank goodness it was two doors down and the probability of Drake hearing anything was slight.

In the dim light of the coach, she noted Charlotte's knee bobbing ever so slightly beneath her skirts. Isadora summoned her courage and flickered her gaze between Drake and Charlotte. Neither looked comfortable. "Drake, are you still planning to join Minerva and me for tea tomorrow?"

"No." Drake stared at Charlotte and continued, "I've decided to go on a Grand Tour now that it is somewhat safe to travel once more. I will be busy making arrangements."

"There is no need for games or lies amongst the four of us." Tom sighed. "Drake refuses to challenge Minerva."

Isadora glared at Drake. "Why are you such a stubborn mule?"

"Minerva deserves a husband to grant her every wish...and I'm simply not that man." He crossed his arms and looked at the coach windows. "The Crown can banish me wherever it pleases,

160

but I cannot marry your sister."

Silence descended upon the coach.

The warmth of Tom's touch long gone, Isadora pulled her cloak tighter about her. "Will you be back in time for my wedding?"

Drake's eyes went wide. "Wedding?"

"Aye. His Grace proposed this eve, and I accepted."

Charlotte patted Isadora's knee. "Drake cannot simply return when he wishes. That is not how things work."

Isadora looked at Tom. "I swore I wouldn't marry before Minerva. We have... A hundred days. A hundred days to find Minerva a husband."

"A hundred days?" Both Tom and Drake repeated simultaneously.

"Aye, we have ninety days in which to hold the ceremony after the banns have been read for three consecutive weeks." Pleased with her concise explanation, Isadora glanced about the coach at its occupants. "A hundred days."

Three sets of bewildered eyes looked back at her. What was the problem?

Drake scowled at her. "Minerva won't like you interfering with her plans."

"Mayhap, but since you will be traveling, I shall manage my sister."

Charlotte looked to Drake and then to Tom. The siblings were communicating again. Would she be privy to their code once she married Tom?

Tom exhaled and said, "I appreciate all your efforts, Charlotte, but no, we will not be marrying by special license. We shall instead assist Isadora in finding Minerva a suitable husband."

Her heart leapt. Tom had backed her request. Perhaps Lady Luck was on her side this eve, for why else had she been blessed with such an understanding and supportive fiancé?

Charlotte nodded. "Very well. I shall begin compiling a list first thing in the morn." Her future sister-in-law reached out and gave Isadora's hands a squeeze. It would be nice to have another sister, one she wouldn't have to keep secrets from. Once she married Tom, she'd no longer be able to share her activities with Minerva or Diana. It would place them in jeopardy.

Drake stiffened in his seat. "Who do you have in mind?"

"It is of no concern of yours," Tom answered. "And it appears you shall miss both Minerva and Isadora's weddings. Shame, considering how close you are to the Malbury family."

The poignant sentiment hit Isadora in the chest. Anger, frustration, and disappointment all rolled through her at once. She pinned Drake with a stare. "Whatever your reasoning is for not complying, it had best be worth it to you."

The coach rolled to a stop, and Isadora quickly gathered her skirts to exit before Drake could respond. But Charlotte placed a hand out to stop her. She peeked out as the coach door opened. They weren't at the Malbury townhouse. They were in front of Drake's residence.

What the devil was going on?

Tom nudged Drake. "Time to pack. I shall assist."

Drake shuffled out the door without a word or a backward glance. Tom followed but stuck his head back in. "I shall meet you both at Lord Torrance's."

Confused, Isadora waited for the coach door to close before asking, "Why am I going to Lord Torrance's residence?"

Charlotte shrugged. "We simply follow orders, not make them."

Isadora sat back as the coach lurched forward. This would be her first insight into what her life would be like once she married Tom.

CHAPTER TWENTY-FIVE

CANDLELIGHT SEEPED BENEATH the drawing room door of Lord Torrance's modest townhome. Tom crept toward the room Isadora was ensconced in. Guilt plagued him. He should have explained to Isadora that it wasn't in his full control to delay their vows. Instead, he let her believe they could play matchmaker for Minerva without consequence. He was a coward.

Ear pressed to the thick wood panel, Tom waited a moment.

Lord Torrance's warm baritone voice filtered through the door. "Lady Isadora, I understand your plight. But we must act swiftly on the information Avondale and Lady Charlotte recently obtained. I cannot in good conscience send you abroad with Avondale without the two of you first being wed."

"My sister has taken great care of my family. She deserves happiness and a family of her own. I will not marry before her." Isadora's tone was resolute.

Tom winced in anticipation of his handler's response, but when Lord Torrance remained silent, Tom placed a hand on the door handle—ready to enter at any moment.

"Lady Isadora, let me be clear—we do not tolerate insubordination within the Foreign Office. There are consequences."

"Until Tom and I are wed, I'm not officially a part of such an organization. My family comes first."

"Oh, for goodness' sake, Your Grace, stop milling about and

enter," Lord Torrance ordered.

He opened the door and smiled at the sight of Isadora standing toe-to-toe with the man that was like a father to him. "Beg pardon for my late arrival."

"Of all the women who have crossed your path..." Lord Torrance said, staring at his intended, "You have chosen wisely."

Tom agreed wholeheartedly. He entered the room and stopped at the sight of Charlotte laid out upon the settee, hands tucked under her cheek with a thick blanket covering her as she slumbered. Since they arrived home from France, his sister had not stopped running from one errand to the next. He should have assisted her more rather than brooding in his rooms over Isadora. He walked over to his sister and tucked the blanket around her.

Eyes closed, Charlotte hissed, "Go away, you will draw their attention to me!"

"I should have known you were feigning," Tom whispered back. He planted a kiss on the top of Charlotte's head, which she rarely let him do anymore.

Tom wiped the smile from his face and turned around to join Torrance and Isadora by the fire. "What has been decided?"

"Nothing." The pair said in unison, and they both continued to glare at each other.

Isadora was magnificent, and the crinkle at the corner of Torrance's eyes told Tom, Torrance agreed.

He wrapped an arm about Isadora's waist and faced Torrance. "There must be a reasonable solution."

"I have tried to convey to your intended here the import of the two of you marrying immediately. Your aunt and I made a great number of promises in order to obtain the special license."

"I appreciate the lengths you have gone to in order to see to Tom's happiness." Isadora leaned in and placed a chaste kiss upon Tom's cheek. "However, I will not yield. Minerva is more important to me than my own welfare." She spun from Tom's hold and began to pace.

Tom opened his mouth to respond when Torrance nudged

him in his back and shook his head. They watched as Isadora muttered to herself, proposing and then discarding various schemes attempting to balance out everyone's goals until she came to a stop mid-turn. "Aha."

The corners of Torrance's mouth twitched. "This should be enlightening."

Isadora came to stand before Tom and tugged on his lapel. "Your Aunt is famed for her matchmaking abilities. She must have a running list of eligible bachelors. We will host an engagement party and invite them all."

"But Minerva has declared she will only marry the man who can defeat her in chess. That is no easy feat." Tom glanced at Torrance for assistance, but his mentor simply shrugged.

"I shall recruit my brother-in-law's help." Isadora's eyes were bright and filled with hope. "We can develop a set of signals, and Chestwick can assist the gentleman. If Minerva believes her opponent to be worthy and he can charm her, she will allow him to defeat her, and voila she'll be engaged and married in short order."

"You're willing to trick your own sister into marriage?" Torrance asked.

"I cannot trick Minerva. She is far too smart for that, but she currently believes she lacks options. We simply need to show her she has the pick of the litter, so to speak."

Tom chuckled, "I'm not certain I care for your reference to my peers as hounds, nor do I follow your plan entirely, however, I believe in you, and thus we should attempt it." If it worked, it would mean Isadora would be his wife sooner rather than later.

He was rewarded with a kiss, and when Isadora was done kissing him, she pulled back and said, "Charlotte you can stop pretending to slumber. What do you think of my plan?"

Charlotte stood and brushed a hand over her rumpled dress. "I like Lady Minerva. If marriage is truly what she wishes, then I say we have much to do."

Torrance cleared his throat. "What about Drake?"

"What about the fool?" Isadora asked.

Torrance deemed Drake the only man in England who possessed the talent to defeat Lady Minerva. In addition, his wife, Lady Ethel firmly believed the pair were unequivocally in love. Torrance asked Isadora, "Would you recommend I send Drake away so he doesn't interfere or allow him to remain?"

"Do as you see fit." Isadora whirled to join Charlotte. "How long do you suppose it will take to arrange everything?"

Charlotte looked over Isadora's shoulder to Torrance. Tom willed and silently begged his mentor to raise no more than two fingers, and as luck would have it, Torrance unfurled two fingers.

His sister sighed and said, "No more than a fortnight."

Tom wanted to jump for joy. He'd have Isadora as wife in two weeks. Surely, he possessed enough strength to contain his adoration for fourteen days, but when Isadora turned to give him a wink and a smile, his resolve crumbled. He'd wait to take her maidenhead, but there were several other ways they could explore pleasure together.

Charlotte let out a squeal, capturing Tom by surprise. Isadora had thrown her arms about his sister. "I shall have to relinquish my role as the patroness of the Wicked Ladies Salon. Will you accept the position if the members approve?"

Charlotte returned Isadora's hug with enthusiasm. "Oh yes! I would love to."

"I know I'd be leaving them in good hands, although I'm a tad sad I'll not be able to participate in the events this Season."

"No need to be sad. I'm certain Tom will ensure you have a wicked time in France."

The ladies linked arms and proceeded to leave the room, leaving Tom alone with Torrance.

"Inform me of what you need, and I'll see that it is done," Torrance said as he slung an arm over Tom's shoulder.

"A case of brandy to start."

Torrance laughed and patted him heartily on the back. "I'll have it delivered by first light."

"Do you believe Isadora's scheme will succeed?"

"Aye, I believe the future Duchess of Avondale will and can accomplish anything she sets her mind to." Torrance motioned for Tom to precede him through the door. "I approve of your choice, and so will the head of the Foreign Office."

Tom sighed. "Two weeks."

"It's a far cry better than one hundred days and nights."

"Aye, you're right." Tom accepted his coat from the butler, waiting in the wings. "Shall I report back in the morn?"

"Nay, get some rest and keep an eye on Drake."

"So, he may remain on home soil?"

"For now." Torrance waved him out the door. "Don't worry about informing him tonight. Escort the ladies home, and I'll send round a note to Captain Bane to inform him he may give Drake the option."

Tom entered the coach. He debated with his conscience whether or not to inform Drake he was no longer being forced to leave. He'd never ignored Torrance's advice before, and he wasn't going to start now.

Seated across from Isadora, an epiphany hit him: Love was a choice.

EPILOGUE

Four weeks later...
Paris, France

SHEATHED INSIDE HIS wife, Tom's hips rolled forward in time with the swell. He would never tire of pleasuring his wife until she reached her climax. It was a sight to behold. Married a month, and he still wanted her every day. Isadora had become a vixen in bed, and he loved every moment they shared abed. She sated a wild desire within him that he had not known even existed. He plunged deeper, and Isadora's moans of pleasure had him increasing the pace of his thrusts.

"Husband, slow down." Isadora pleaded.

He granted her wish and rubbed his thumb in a circular motion over the soft mound that he knew would bring her closer to release.

"Thomas Grandst...stone—I love you." Isadora pushed up her hips to meet his thrusts.

He loved the way she always proclaimed her love for him when she was on the cusp of climax. He continued to drive into her over and over until he found his own release.

Exhausted, he rolled to lay on his side next to Isadora on the bunk barely large enough to accommodate them both. Most nights, Isadora slept upon him, which he didn't mind in the least.

He often found himself waking with his wife straddled across his hips, his cock alive, buried in between her lovely thighs as she rocked in time to waves.

Isadora yawned. "Before we fall asleep, I want to thank you for marrying me and allowing me to accompany you on these missions. You fill my heart and soul with joy."

"I never thought I'd say these words. In fact, I swore after my parents' death I would never allow my wife to join me in such dangerous activities for the Crown, but now I understand why my papa insisted on my mama's company. My heart would be sliced in half if you were not by my side. I love you with every fiber of my being, Isadora, and you won't be rid of me any time soon."

Rolling to her side and snuggling closer, Isadora closed her eyes and said, "I love you, too, husband."

Want to find out how Isadora's scheme to see Minerva wed first worked? Find out in King takes Queen.

About the Author

Rachel Ann Smith writes steamy historical romances with a twist. Her debut series, Agents of the Home Office, features female protagonists that defy convention.

When Rachel isn't writing, she loves to read and spend time with the family. She is frequently found with her Kindle by the pool during the summer, on the side-lines of the soccer field in the spring and fall or curled up on the couch during the winter months.

She currently lives in Colorado with her extremely understanding husband and their two very supportive children.

Visit Rachel's website for updates on cover reveals and new releases – www.rachelannsmith.com.

You can also stay up to date with Rachel following her on social media.

Facebook: rachelannsmit11
BookBub: bookbub.com/authors/rachel-ann-smith
Amazon: amazon.com/Rachel-Ann-Smith/e/B07THSRH6B
Twitter: @rachelannsmit11
Instagram: instagram.com/rachelannsmithauthor
Goodreads:
goodreads.com/author/show/19301975.Rachel_Ann_Smith

9 781958 098127